SPELL OF THE WEREWOLF

J.R. LOVELESS

J.R. LOVELESS PUBLISHING

SPELL OF THE WEREWOLF

By J.R. Loveless

Two centuries ago, Justin was turned against his will into a werewolf - a mindless, angry beast three nights a month. Ever since, he has done everything he can to atone for the blood on his hands, even going so far as to hunt his own kind. The burden of carrying on is heavy and unforgiving, and he's reached the point of not caring if he lives or dies.

Vincent is a hybrid, half-werewolf and half-human, spending his days, and nights, hunting werewolves. Vincent may be half-monster, but he lives and breathes by his human half. Hunting werewolves and taking down as many of the creatures as possible is all he can see.

A chance meeting changes everything. A deal struck between them, a threat to humanity, and their mutual attraction combined brings them together in an explosive way. Vincent has found the one who can break down the walls around his heart – will he now be able to carry through on his promise to end Justin's torment, or will Justin live to see another moonrise?

CHAPTER 1

The crunching of bones breaking and mending echoed off the cement walls and metal cage surrounding him, while his gasps of pain mingled with the excruciating change until Justin lay there a panting, trembling mess. He curled into a fetal position, staring at the bars and wondering how much longer he could continue to live through the unbearable transformation. Every full moon he became a monster with no thought of anything except feasting on flesh, human or otherwise. He'd lock himself in a steel cage lined with silver in the basement of whatever house they were renting to stop himself from hurting anyone on the three nights he couldn't control himself.

"You're back to normal, I see." A low voice came through the darkness.

Justin closed his eyes against the brightness of the light flicked on and Kara, his best friend and caretaker, stepped toward the cage with keys in hand. She unlocked the door, then the chains, and helped him to his feet. After handing him his clothing, she went back upstairs without another word. Kara was the only person in his life who knew about the beast inside of him. She'd been a loyal friend and his only family for the last ten years. But before her, he'd spent almost two hundred years on his own, merely surviving.

Despite his outward appearance of an eighteen-year-old young man, he'd actually lived for two hundred and eighteen years. He stood at an even six foot with a wiry, lean build, which never changed no matter what he ate or how much he exercised. Black hair, as dark as a moonless night, just brushed his shoulders when he didn't keep it tied back. Most humans found it hard to stare into his eerily light blue eyes. Maybe because they could sense the evil lurking beneath the surface, or perhaps they could see the creature pacing inside him, waiting for the nights it could be free.

In the time since his life changed forever, he'd seen many wonderful and horrible things: the invention of trains, cars, and airplanes, wars, slavery, death, and blood. The only cure he knew of to end his torment was either death or to kill the one who'd bitten him. His desperate search led him here, to Japan, where he spent every waking hour not working trying to find word of the bastard's whereabouts.

Justin made his way upstairs to the kitchen and found Kara cooking breakfast on the old stove in the house they'd rented. He watched her as she moved about the tiny kitchen. Petite at five-foot-two, she had beautiful auburn hair that hung down her back to her hourglass waist. She kept it in a ponytail most of the time. Bright green eyes complimented the light dusting of freckles across her nose. He cared for her a great deal, even loved her in his own way, but he knew it wasn't the kind of love she wanted from him.

Thirty-five now, she'd found him ten years ago lying in the bushes in her backyard the morning after a full moon. He'd had large wounds all over his body from a fight he'd been in with another werewolf in the area. She'd tended his injuries and taken care of him until he'd regained consciousness. When he'd awakened, she'd demanded the story from him; she said it was either that or she'd call the police. So he'd told her everything, his past and the monster hiding beneath his flesh. They'd been together ever since, moving from place to place in search of the one who could break his curse. They both worked odd jobs during the day to support them as they moved from city to city and country to country. It'd been her idea to build the cage lined with silver and secure it to the ground wherever they were.

Setting a plate on the table for him and another for herself, she slid into one of the chairs. "You were overly anxious last night. More so than usual."

Justin looked at her and then away. He picked up his fork but didn't begin eating immediately. "I don't remember anything, you know that, Kara. Maybe there's another werewolf close by."

There were many malevolent creatures in the world that humans remained unaware of, or they chose to ignore the obvious signs, writing off anything unexplained as animal attacks. Mostly, his kind stayed away from one another unless they felt threatened. "Tonight's the last full moon, for this month at least. I don't know how much longer I can take this, Kara. I want it to be over."

Kara studied him for a long moment before replying, "We'll find him, Justin. You just need to have patience."

"How much more patience can I have, Kara?" Justin snapped. "It's been two hundred years. Another hundred and I'll go insane!"

She looked at him sadly but didn't say anything. They sat in silence for the remainder of breakfast. Justin barely touched the scrambled eggs, attempting a bite or two to appease Kara, but he couldn't stomach the idea of eating. He knew she meant well, and she couldn't really understand why he wanted to die, but her words only served to reinforce why he couldn't continue to live like this.

After breakfast, Kara washed the dishes and then grabbed her purse. "I'm on my way to work. I'll be back before the sun sets to lock you in."

He watched her leave, staying at the table even after she'd gone. The night he'd been bitten played in his head like a mini movie, almost as if it were someone else's reality. It was 1802, and he'd been out drinking at a local tavern, celebrating the birth of his best friend's baby. When the owner finally kicked them out at two in the morning, he started toward home, weaving along the street in his drunkenness. Most people were tucked in their beds asleep. No noises could be heard other than the odd stray cat in the alley garbage bins or the lone bark of a dog in the far off distance. A loud crashing sound echoed off the cobblestones and in between buildings just before a large heavy weight slammed into him. He flew through the air, landing with a thud on the unforgiving street.

He realized a huge animal, something akin to a wild dog, lay on top of him, pinning him to the ground. Before he could react, the animal sank his teeth into his shoulder. Justin remembered screaming in pain as blood poured from the torn flesh. He heard a gunshot as someone came running down the street, yelling to scare off the dog. The animal let go and ran off, leaving him lying in a pool of his own blood.

The man who'd saved him had taken Justin to his home and rung the doctor. The doctor stitched him up and bandaged his wound. Justin returned to his own home the next day and went about his normal life. The wound healed in a miraculously short amount of time, and he'd begun to notice strange things happening to his body in the following weeks. He found himself abnormally attracted to the scent of blood, and he could smell things from several hundred feet away. His eye sight and hearing grew sharper, and his strength increased three fold.

The first full moon came a little over three weeks after he'd been bitten. He was out chopping firewood for his parents when it started. He thanked God every day since then that he hadn't been home when it happened. He remembered dropping to his knees as a sudden pain gripped his entire body. His screams of anguish filled the forest behind his home; the snapping of his bones breaking was the only thing louder than his cries. Hair sprouted along his hands and arms; his jaw elongated into a snout. He could still feel the terror he'd felt during his first change. He lost consciousness afterward or so he'd thought. He figured out the next morning that when he became the monster inside, he lost all control of his awareness and the beast took over.

The only thing he remembered was waking up covered in blood the next morning. He'd vomited at the grisly sight beside him. A mutilated body of a man lay near him. He couldn't even identify the face of the man, to know who he'd been, because his face had been torn to shreds and then gnawed on by some great animal. He'd gone to the nearby river to wash the blood away the best he could and made his way slowly toward home, where he'd snuck into his room to pack some of his things. He left a note for his parents telling them he was sorry, but he could no longer stay with them. They weren't safe with him. He'd saddled his horse and left for good.

He'd been running ever since. The only person he'd gotten close to in the last two hundred years was Kara. Even after ten years he still feared for her safety, but she never let him take off alone no matter how many times he tried.

Pushing up from the table, he went to get ready to head to his job. He worked as a waiter at a nearby sushi restaurant. When he finished showering and getting dressed, he snatched his keys from the hook and stuffed his feet into his shoes by the door. Outside, the sun shone brightly overhead, hurting his eyes, and he slid his usual pair of sunglasses on as he climbed onto a black motorcycle sitting at the edge of the curb. The engine started with a low purr, and he took off down the street, darting into the rush-hour traffic on the main street.

Arriving at the restaurant, he found his boss, Lee, in a panic. "What's going on, Lee?" Justin greeted him.

"Justin, great, you're here. I need your help. The hostess called out today, and you're the only one with full experience to take care of the front. You're on Maître d' duty today."

Justin sighed and scowled. He hated running the hostess stand. It didn't bring in any tips, but he needed the job as long as they were in Japan. So he nodded at Lee and went to the back to change into one of the spare host outfits they kept in the back. The first hour progressed uneventfully, mostly table settings and prepping for the day. Lunchtime tended to be their busiest time. Before long the restaurant became crowded, and Justin didn't have a spare minute to think. He felt exhausted by the time the lunch rush ended, and he snuck out to the alley behind the restaurant for a five-minute cigarette break.

Happily dragging on the cigarette, he felt the nicotine fill his veins and breathed in relief. A sound at the end of the alley caught his attention, and he saw a man standing there, watching him. Justin narrowed his eyes at the stranger, staring him down, and wondered what the man's problem was. Admittedly gorgeous, the stranger appeared to be a few inches taller than his six foot with a head full of white hair, which hung over one shoulder in a braid straight down to his waist. Justin's keen gaze could make out the deepest violet eyes he'd ever seen.

Justin felt an odd tingle of foreboding trickle down his spine the longer they stared at one another. Tossing his cigarette on the ground, he stomped it out with his boot and went inside, ignoring the man's eyes boring into his back. He returned to the front to relieve Kaito, the only other host backup, and he almost gasped out loud in shock. The man from outside stood waiting for a table, and a beautiful woman with bright blonde hair stood next to him. "A table for two, please," she murmured.

"This way." Justin once again felt the man's gaze burning into the nape of his neck and shrugged his shoulders to try and release the tension in them.

He seated the couple, glanced at Hitomi to get her attention for the new patrons, and returned to the host stand. Every once in a while, Justin could feel the man's eyes on him, but he studiously refused to look at him. He didn't know what the stranger's problem was, but it wasn't his to take on. By late afternoon he knew he had to leave soon, or he'd be caught outside when the change began. The second he felt his skin start to itch, Justin realized he had to go. The beast lurked beneath the surface, pacing restlessly. The first night of the full moon the shift took over an hour, but with each successive night, it happened faster and sooner. By the third night, it no longer needed the moon to be high overhead when it came.

He went to his boss and told him he had to leave.

"I need you to stay, Justin," Lee replied sternly.

"I can't. You know that, Lee." Justin didn't say anything further, immediately heading into the back of the restaurant to change into his street clothes. He left through the rear entrance, went to where he'd parked, and slid onto his motorcycle. He saw the same white-haired man leaning against a building nearby as he started the engine, and Justin glared at him as he zipped into traffic toward home.

The sun hung low in the sky, and with each passing minute Justin could feel the beast pressing in on him, clawing at his skin to be free. Kara pulled up to the house just as Justin rounded the corner of their street. He barely took the time to turn off the bike before dismounting. "Hurry," he told her.

The sun sank below the horizon, moving quickly. He could feel the sensation of electricity dancing along his nerves, and sweat beaded on his brow as they rushed into the house and down the basement stairs. Kara just managed to get the lock clicked into place when the change began.

CHAPTER 2

The moon rose higher into the sky the longer Vincent waited outside the house of the boy he'd seen at the restaurant. He'd followed him home and seen him meet with a petite red-headed woman out front. He held his swords with both hands in preparation for the beast to come charging out of the house, but as the time passed and nothing happened, he realized the animal didn't appear to be going on their usual rampage. Confusion creased his forehead. He could have sworn the younger man was one of them. Why hadn't he already changed?

Vincent slid his swords into their sheaths, creeping closer to the house. He found a window that looked into the kitchen, and he saw the woman from before slumped near a door, crying. He stopped and listened. There! The sounds of a wild beast howling and raging could be heard from inside, but it sounded as though it were caged. He frowned and headed around the house toward the noise. A small window, spotted with dirt, looked in on a basement. Vincent's eyes widened in surprise when he saw the beast was, in fact, in a cage. Its huge paws pulled at the bars with impossible strength, but it only held on for a short moment before wrenching away, seemingly in pain. The animal threw its head back and howled with rage, rattling the door again.

He needed to get in there. Heading around to the front of the house, he tried the doorknob but found it locked. Growling in frustration, he knocked on the door. A couple minutes went by and then the woman cracked open the door and asked rudely, "What do you want?"

Before she could stop him, he shoved his way inside, slamming the door behind him. She launched herself at him and tried to prevent him from getting any further into the house. Vincent batted her away like a fly. The sound of her grunt of pain when she hit the floor didn't even phase him.

"What are you doing here?" she screamed, struggling to her feet again.

He ignored her and strode through to the door he'd seen her leaning against. Flicking on the light as he took the stairs two at a time, he saw the beast pacing the cage. Vincent sneered in disgust. Werewolves were one of the nastiest creatures in the preternatural world, driven only by their animalistic need for flesh and blood. Unlike typical shifters, werewolves stood on two legs, and they became nothing but the animal they shifted into. They lost all sense of their humanity. The one before him topped out at seven and a half feet with black fur and massive paws. Razor sharp claws glinted in the moonlight every time the beast attempted to grab hold of the bars, trying to break free, and saliva dripped from the three inch fangs protruding out of the elongated jaws.

When the werewolf saw him, it went into a frenzy, raging at him and trying to break free from its prison. Vincent pulled one sword from its sheath. His swords, made from pure silver, had been used to kill many of these monsters over the years. He approached the cage and was about to slide the blade through the bars toward the beast's heart when he heard a gun cock behind him.

"If you don't get the hell out of here right now I'm going to shoot you, mister."

Vincent pulled the sword back and looked over his shoulder toward the woman standing at the bottom of the stairs with a deadly looking pistol aimed at him. He knew it wouldn't kill him, but it sure as hell would hurt. "Why are you protecting him?" he demanded.

"Because he's my friend and because he doesn't deserve to die for something he has no control over," the woman stated flatly. "He didn't ask to become what he is. He's trying to find the one who bit him, to end the curse."

"You're not doing him any good. The more he is denied the taste of flesh, the more dangerous he becomes," Vincent told her coldly.

"It's worked for ten years. Now get out of my house before I shoot you," she threatened again, her finger tightening a fraction on the trigger.

Vincent stared at her, curious as to why she cared so much about a snarling, slavering beast that would kill her without a single ounce of remorse if it ever got free. He knew he could kill the creature before she could get off more than one shot, but instead he bowed his head and walked around her, up the steps, and out of the house. He wouldn't risk harming a human.

~

The next morning, Kara told Justin about the white-haired man who'd come to kill him. "I knew there was something weird about the way he watched me at the restaurant," Justin mused, mostly to himself.

"What? He knows where you work? You can't go back there, Justin!"

"I need the job, Kara. If we don't have money we can't stay here, and I can't find *him*."

"But he'll kill you," Kara said vehemently.

"Maybe it would be better if he did."

Justin ignored her gasp of shock and went into his room to get ready for work. He knew she didn't understand why he wouldn't run. What was the point? He'd spent most of his life running, looking for that one needle in a haystack, searching to find a ghost practically. There were always whispers, rumors of the one who'd bit him, but it never panned out into more than disappointment.

Fully dressed, he left his bedroom and grabbed his keys on the way out the door. He glanced around him as he walked out of the house, wondering if the man from yesterday would be there, watching and waiting for him, but he didn't see or sense anyone outside. A slight sigh of relief left him as he climbed onto his bike and started the engine. Everything passed by him in a blur, his mind still on the events of the day before. When he reached the restaurant, he found out the hostess had taken another sick day, and he would have to be up front again. He shook his head in resignation. Being the host gave him too much time to think. The lunch rush came, giving him a couple of hours where he was too busy to brood over his life, but after it calmed down, his mind went back into overdrive. Stepping out into the back alley for a smoke break, he flicked his lighter, touching the flame to the end of the cigarette.

The smells in the alley were almost overpowering today. He wrinkled his nose in disgust and took a deep drag before breathing out slowly. *Maybe it would be better if he killed me*, Justin thought to himself. *I'm tired of living. Kara is wasting her life, and my entire family is dead. What's the point of still being here? To spend eternity alone?*

Kara's smiling face came to mind, and the same regret he'd felt since the day he'd wound up in her yard filled him. She wouldn't let him go off alone. When he attempted to leave her behind, she simply followed. He'd tried more than once to convince her to go back to her life, but she'd just smack him for being stupid and go about taking care of him. His lips curved in an affectionate smile. He really did care about her.

A slight breeze kicked up through the alley and he tensed, catching the scent of another werewolf. He narrowed his eyes and approached the end of the alley to look around for the source. He saw a man across the street who moved in a way only his kind could. Crossing the street, he followed the stranger. The scent didn't belong to the one who'd bitten him, but in the past two centuries he'd taken out quite a number of the beasts in search of him.

The werewolf stopped to look around, making sure no one followed him, and then slipped into another passageway. Justin pursued him single-mindedly. Once they were far enough away from the street so as not to draw attention to them, Justin said, "You're getting sloppy. You couldn't even tell I was behind you."

Swinging around in surprise, the creature stared at him, eyes flashing yellow. "You!" he snarled, hatred buried in the dark irises. "I've heard of you. One of us, yet you hunt us."

"I am nothing like you," Justin growled, clenching his fists at his side. "You're a monster, a killer."

The man snorted. "And what makes you so different, boy? Because you kill your own kind? You're still a werewolf inside. You still change on the full moon. Too bad you chose to pick a fight with me. I think I'll take your head and wear it as a trophy."

Justin opened his mouth to snap back, but no words came out. Before his very eyes, the man began to change. Without a full moon! Justin reared back in shock and horror. He couldn't believe it. Their kind could only shift during a full moon, not in broad daylight in the middle of the city! Within seconds, rather than the thirty minutes to an hour the change could normally take, the creature stood in front of Justin in all his glory, seven feet of hairy, hulking flesh. Saliva dripped from the long fangs Justin knew too well. Justin reached down to grab the gun loaded with silver bullets that he kept strapped to his leg under his jeans. He straightened, bringing his hand up at the same time, but it was too late, the creature had already launched himself at Justin.

The werewolf backhanded the gun out of his hand and grabbed his throat. Justin's eyes widened in surprise. The beast seemed to have conscious thought despite having shifted. Justin found himself flying through the air for a split second before slamming into the wall and tumbling down to the cement. Several bricks knocked loose from the building rained down around him as he dragged himself to his feet. He saw his gun lying on the ground by the beast's clawed toes, but there was no way he'd be able to get to it.

The werewolf moved toward him, a purposeful look in the glaring yellow eyes. Just as he went to reach for Justin again, a figure landed next to them, crouching down with a huge silver sword arced out behind him, blood dripping from the blade. If the situation had been different, Justin may have laughed at the incredulous expression on the werewolf's face as he realized the truth. The sword had sliced clean through his neck, and gravity hadn't quite caught up just yet. His eyes rolled back as his head lolled to the side and separated from his body. The loud thud of the corpse hitting the concrete echoed along the side of the buildings.

Justin moved with preternatural speed to snatch his gun from where it lay, swinging around to point the barrel at the white-haired stranger from the day before. "Who are you, and what the hell do you want?"

Smirking, the man leaned against the side of the building. "So you're the one the others talk about."

CHAPTER 3

J ustin stared at him and repeated the questions. "Who are you? What do you want?"

"My name is Vincent, and I want you dead." He pointed his sword at Justin. "I just want to know why you're hunting your own kind?"

"My own kind? I've *never* been like those monsters," Justin said bitterly.

"Except three nights a month, right?" Vincent challenged.

Despair, regret, and pain swamped Justin, and he was pretty sure Vincent could see his emotions on his face, if not in his eyes. "I didn't ask to be this way, you know. I was attacked by some monster and not given a choice."

"You could have killed yourself," Vincent pointed out.

"You think I haven't tried?" Justin demanded in anguish. "Every time I attempt to, Kara finds a way to stop me."

"Kara? Ah, the girl from last night. Your protector," Vincent sneered at him. "How sweet. A human protecting a werewolf."

Justin got angry. "Leave her alone. You know nothing about her or me. If you're going to try and kill me, get it over with before you bore me to death with your talking. I have to get back to work."

Vincent raised his sword and advanced on him, but in the blink of an eye, Justin leapt into the air and grabbed the fire escape. He hauled himself up onto the metal stairs and started running up them. The metal clanged loudly beneath his feet, and he could hear Vincent in pursuit behind him. Reaching the roof, Justin raced to the edge and bounded across to the other building. Vincent couldn't follow him there, or so he thought.

His breath caught when Vincent jumped over to the other building with ease. The man's impact on the roof caused it to crack in several places around him. Pushing back his trench coat from his crouched position, Vincent drew his sword again and stood.

"What are you?" Justin asked incredulously, backing away.

"I'm what you'd call… a hybrid. Part human, part werewolf. Without the nasty beast side three times a month." Vincent advanced toward him and watched as Justin retreated.

"So you hunt your own kind then?" Justin challenged.

"Touché."

Justin continued inching his way to the other side only to stop when his knees hit the edge. "All out of roof, wolf." Vincent smiled in triumph.

Closing his eyes, Justin pushed himself backward off the building. He flipped over in midair and landed with both feet under him. He smirked at Vincent peering at him over the ledge and gave him the middle finger before darting down the alley to the street, bursting out into the crowds on the sidewalk. Immediately, he headed back to the restaurant, knowing Lee would be pissed.

His theory proved correct. The moment he walked in the door, Lee demanded to know where he was at. "I'm sorry, Lee. Something came up, and I had to take care of it really quick. I was only gone for a half hour."

Lee shook his head and glared at him. "Don't do it again." He spun on his heel and went into his office.

Asshole, Justin thought to himself and forced a smile for the next person who came in the front door.

Later in the afternoon, he left work and breathed a sigh into the early twilight air. This was the first night after the full moon where he would remain human. He decided to go for a ride on his motorcycle before going home. The streets were littered with tourists and residents of Tokyo. He looked at the sights around him as he drove. His mind went back to the events of earlier in the day. How the hell did that werewolf change in the middle of the day? And how was it possible for him to have conscious thought while in his wolf form? Justin's thoughts went around and around, unable to find the answer.

When he reached the house there were no lights on, and he frowned as he dismounted his bike. Where was Kara? The front door stood slightly ajar, and panic began to set in. Maybe one of the werewolves had found out where they lived. They knew he hunted and destroyed them. He found nothing disturbed within the house as he crept through the entry and into the kitchen, searching for Kara. He noticed a small dagger stuck in a wall in the kitchen with a piece of paper. Grabbing the knife, he yanked the point from the wall and snatched the paper before it could hit the floor.

I have your friend, wolf. If you ever want to see her alive again, you'll be at Wadakura Fountain Park at seven o'clock.

Justin growled and crumpled the paper in his hand. So the asshole wanted to threaten Kara. Justin slammed into his bedroom and pulled out the sword he'd banished to the trunk in his closet a long time ago. He'd sworn to never use it again, but Kara needed him. He changed out of his work clothes into a pair of dark-washed jeans and a tight white tank top with a black jean jacket and stuffed his feet into black combat boots. The ruby stud earring in his left ear glinted in the nearby mirror as he tied his hair back from his face with a bit of string.

After sliding the sword into a duffle, he strapped the bag to his back and stormed from the house to his motorcycle. The waning moon hung above him as he revved the engine of his bike before streaking off from the curb. All he could do was pray Kara hadn't been hurt. Rage boiled through him, rippling beneath his skin and through his veins. Wind whipped at his clothing and hair. The sword bounced against him when he hit small bumps in the road, reminding him of the heavy presence. His heart thudded harder when the park came into view.

Stopping his motorcycle, he got off and kept to the shadow of the trees, attempting to remain unseen until he'd scouted the situation. Kara sat on the edge of the fountain with Vincent only a matter of feet away. The sound of Kara's voice reached him where he stood.

"Why are you doing this?" Kara demanded.

"I already told you, human. I want him dead."

"Why? What did he ever do to you?"

"Nothing. His kind deserves to die. Every second draws him closer to the murder of another human being," Vincent snapped.

Kara shook her head. "I feel sorry for you."

"Sorry for me?" Vincent gave her an incredulous look. "Why should you feel sorry for me?"

"Because you are so closed-minded you can't see anything but what you want to see. Justin is a good person. He didn't ask to be what he is. We can still find the one who bit him!"

Vincent laughed, a clear cynical sound behind it. "*If* he can find the one who made him. The number of werewolves grows every day. It'll be impossible. So, no. He has to die!"

Justin had heard enough. He stepped forward and called, "Vincent."

Vincent whipped his head around and smiled, harsh and bitter. "So you decided to show. This human means that much to you?"

"Let her go," Justin snarled, ignoring Vincent's question. "Then we can fight."

"I'll let her go... once you're dead."

Justin pulled the sword from his back and moved into the light shining from the fountain. "Let's do it then."

"Ah, so the little boy went and got himself a big knife, did he? Do you even know how to use it?" Vincent taunted him.

He did an expert twist of his wrist, sending the blade of the sword spinning around him. Vincent's eyes narrowed just before he attacked. Their blades clashed against one another as they fought; their movements almost an elegant dance between them. "So you've had some training, kid? It's not enough to save your ass."

Vincent thrust at him, but Justin cut up with his sword and sent Vincent's flying into the air. The blade clattered against the ground, landing a few feet from them. Before Justin could strike at him again, Vincent leapt backward, grabbed his sword, and flipped, landing several yards away from Justin. Justin knew it wasn't going to be an easy fight.

Circling one another, their swords glinted in the moonlight. Justin narrowed his eyes while he waited for Vincent to make the first move. Too impatient to wait for Justin to make his move, Vincent went to strike once more. Justin blocked the blow and attempted a return hit, but Vincent was too fast, crashing his sword into Justin's. Swords crossed at the blade, Justin thrust upward and managed to nick Vincent's cheek. Vincent cursed, jumped backward, and touched the small cut. His fingers were dark with a smear of blood when he dropped his hand from his cheek. Justin smiled mockingly at him. "Aw. Did I cut you?"

Vincent curled his lip into a snarl and rushed toward Justin with his sword raised. The fight continued for some time, and eventually they stood facing one another, panting for breath. Justin could see Vincent's anger reflecting outward from bright violet eyes. He'd never met another person with eyes the shade of amethyst. If he were honest with himself, Vincent would have caught his attention many years ago. The broad shoulders, gorgeous white hair, high cheekbones, and obvious strength rang all of Justin's bells. Of course, the idea of Vincent ever having an interest in him caused Justin to snort.

The sound set off the next chain of events, flaming Vincent's rage even higher, or so Justin figured when Vincent struck harder than before. They circled each other. Vincent took the next chance to slice at Justin, but Justin grabbed his wrist and wrenched him forward and over his shoulder, sending Vincent's sword across the ground to Kara's feet with a clatter of metal on the cement. Justin immediately pinned Vincent underneath him. Breathing heavily, Justin sat there atop Vincent for several seconds without a word, trying to catch his breath.

"I don't want to kill you," Justin rasped.

Vincent looked up at him in skepticism. "Why?" Vincent demanded.

Justin retained eye contact with him. "Because I don't like hurting someone who hates those monsters just as much as I do."

Vincent seemed to contemplate Justin's words, and then something seemed to click inside Vincent. The fight left his body. Justin became aware of Vincent's hard body against his, their suggestive position, and what it could have meant in another world. Flushing, Justin stood and held his hand out to Vincent, who studied him for several heartbeats before allowing Justin's help up from the ground. Justin rushed to Kara's side to untie her hands and massaged them to bring the feeling back into them.

"Don't think this means I trust you, wolf," Vincent growled as he retrieved his sword. "If you even so much as look at a human in the wrong way, I won't hesitate to kill you."

The sound of his sword bottoming out in its sheath punctuated his promise.

Kara glanced at him and snapped, "How do we know we can trust you?"

"You don't." Without another word, he strode off into the darkness.

They watched him disappear and then looked at each other. Justin helped Kara stand, and they headed back to his motorcycle, both lost in their own thoughts of what had taken place mere moments ago. Justin climbed onto the bike and waited for her to slide on behind him. "Justin?"

The bike started with a loud roar. "Yeah?" he responded as he pulled onto the street and made a U-turn toward home.

"You used your sword." Kara shouted into his ear to be heard over the wind rushing by them.

He tensed and rolled his shoulders. His words were almost lost to the breeze as he responded. "I know."

CHAPTER 4

The next day Justin didn't have to work, and so he decided to return to the alley from the day before. He wanted to see if he could find out where the werewolf had been headed. Justin still couldn't fathom how the werewolf had changed without a full moon and how he had retained control of himself once fully wolfed out. There were no traces of the body, and he figured Vincent destroyed all of the evidence. He checked three doors before he reached the end of the alley and realized there was another one, almost hidden from sight. The door would have been rather heavy for a human, but he opened it with little effort. It emitted a high-pitched squeal on the swing inward, the hinges obviously needing oiled. Justin winced, waited to see if the noise drew attention, and then continued on when nothing came charging at him.

Despite the lack of light in the tunnel, his eyes adjusted without issue. He caught the scent of several different werewolves. Frowning in confusion, he crept along the corridor until he heard a hum of some kind. The sound grew louder the closer he got, and then he realized the hum belonged to voices. Lots of them. He'd almost reached the end when another partially open door came into view. He leaned closer, trying to hear what they were saying. They were chanting in another language. One Justin couldn't identify. The stench of various wolves had grown stronger, overpowering, and too hard to separate just how many were in the room.

Justin knew getting caught there, alone, and with only his gun, would be extremely bad. He turned and raced back the way he'd come, keeping his footsteps as light as possible. Bursting out into the sunlight, he slammed his eyes shut in discomfort, the sudden light like thousands of needles jabbing into his eyes at once. He slipped his sunglasses down, and when he opened his eyes he saw Vincent standing at the end of the alley. Justin heard a sound behind him and turned in time to see a huge werewolf exiting the tunnel.

The beast roared at him, spittle raining down on Justin's face. Stunned, Justin didn't move in time and claws slashed across his chest, slicing him open. Justin grunted and slammed into the wall opposite the door. Blood gushed from the wound, soaking his clothing and the ground in front of him. Justin slid down the wall, black dots dancing in front of his eyes. Vincent running toward the two of them was the last thing Justin saw before he passed out, the blessed darkness engulfing him and removing the pain.

~

Vincent saw the werewolf appear in the doorway too late to shout a warning to Justin. He winced when the creature's claws ripped into the other wolf's chest. On the run toward them, he pulled out his swords, and the sound of them being unsheathed caused the beast to turn and face him, roaring in rage. A wild look overtook the werewolf's face before he charged. Claws slashed at Vincent, but he jumped backward and swung his sword. Blood spurted when the blade made contact, slicing the monster's fingers clean off his right hand. A howl of agony shook the brick walls around them.

Using the momentary distraction, he slammed the blade of his sword into the side of the werewolf's neck. The clean, swift swing beheaded the beast instantly, and the head rolled off and landed at Vincent's feet. A second later, the body followed with a loud thud. He sneered in distaste and then turned his attention to Justin. The temptation to kill the boy and be done with him was great, but he wanted answers to what Justin had seen and why he'd been in there to begin with. Scowling, he hefted Justin over his shoulder and began the trek to his apartment. He stuck to back streets and alleys between buildings until he reached his place. The fire escape creaked beneath their combined weight. Thankfully he didn't keep his window locked.

He dropped Justin unceremoniously onto his bed and grabbed some washcloths and bandages. Vincent knew it wouldn't take long for the kid to heal, but it didn't feel right to not clean and cover the wounds for the time being. Setting a bowl of hot water on the nightstand, he perched on the edge of the bed and then proceeded to rip the shirt from Justin's torso. He dipped the washcloth into the water and washed off the blood. The wounds had stopped bleeding but were still gaping open.

Vincent found himself struggling to remain detached. He trailed the washcloth along the cut of Justin's pec, swallowing hard at the expanse of tanned muscles. When he found himself practically caressing Justin's chest, he wrenched his hand away and dropped the cloth into the bowl. He applied the bandages, taped them down, and then went to take a shower.

Hot water tinged with pink ran down his body as Vincent stood there, one arm braced on the shower wall, head bent. His thoughts went in circles over his reaction to Justin's nude form. What the hell was wrong with him? The remembrance of the warm skin beneath his fingers sent arousal through him, causing his cock to harden. To his shame, he found his hand sliding down his abdomen to wrap around his shaft. He squeezed and then began to stroke from tip to base. It didn't take long until he found himself stifling a cry, hard spurts mixing with the water swirling into the drain.

He slumped against the wall, panting and bewildered. Disgust at himself set in. He shoved his long hair back from his face with a sneer. How could he be turned on by a monster? Growling, he turned off the water, snatched a towel from the rack near the shower, and briskly dried his body. He towel-dried his hair, dragged a comb through it several times, and braided it in an expert manner. Tying off the end, he tossed it over his shoulder, wrapped the towel around his waist, and exited the bathroom.

~

J ustin had just sat up, wondering where the hell he was, when Vincent appeared in a nearby doorway. A flush heated his face when he saw Vincent wore nothing but a towel, and he dropped his gaze to his lap. "I see you're finally awake," Vincent said as he opened a closet.

A choke caught in Justin's throat when Vincent dropped the towel, uncaring of his nudity as he dressed in a no nonsense way. The sight of Vincent's firm, rounded ass caused a reaction in Justin's crotch, and he shoved a corner of the blanket he lay on over his rapidly stiffening cock. What the hell was wrong with him? The pale skin of Vincent's body disappeared underneath the clothing Vincent pulled on, much to Justin's horror at his own dismay.

When Vincent finished dressing, he sat down in a chair across from the bed and gave Justin a fierce look. "I want to know what you were doing down the tunnel and what you saw."

Justin knew the only way he could get Vincent to trust him was to tell him everything. So he relayed all of the details about the werewolf scents and the chanting. Justin left out how the chanting had caused a shiver of dread to run down his spine or how it made his insides turn cold. He could see Vincent's surprise over so many wolves in one place. "You're certain there was a pack together in the same room? Did you hear what they were chanting?"

"Yes, I'm certain. I couldn't make out all of the smells, but there were at least eight to ten different scents in the tunnel. The words were unclear, but it sounded like an old kind of language."

Vincent sat there with a pensive look on his face. Justin looked down toward his chest and saw the bandages. He only then realized

Vincent must have done it. Why had Vincent helped him? He could have just as easily killed Justin while he was unconscious. "Why didn't you kill me?" he asked.

Vincent glared at him. "Because you're more useful alive than dead right now."

Disappointment and hurt shafted through Justin, but he hid how Vincent's words made him feel. *Don't be stupid. He couldn't care less about you. You're nothing except a monster to him.* "I see."

Justin slowly pushed himself off the bed and began to remove the bandages. The gashes had pretty much healed by then. The only blemishes left were deep pink lines running across his chest. Within another fifteen minutes even those would be gone. When he went to leave, Vincent stopped him. "You probably should put on a shirt to avoid drawing attention to yourself."

Hand hovering on the knob, Justin hesitated but then turned with a stiff, "Thanks."

He grabbed one at random and slid it over his head. The shirt was a bit baggy on him, as Vincent's shoulders were broader than his own. The scent of Vincent enveloped Justin, and he shivered at how intimate wearing Vincent's shirt felt. With a curt nod toward the hybrid, Justin opened the studio apartment door and left.

Once on the sidewalk, he started running, wanting to escape the sensual thoughts running through his brain and the way Vincent stirred things inside of him that he hadn't felt in years, if ever. But no matter how hard or how fast he ran, Vincent's scent clung to the material encasing his chest, keeping the lust ignited in his veins.

Justin stripped the shirt from himself the moment he entered the house. He could sense Kara wasn't home as he strode bare-chested down the hallway to his bedroom. Tossing the shirt into the corner of his room, as far as possible from him, he moved to the bed and collapsed on top of his covers. Within minutes he'd passed out, exhausted from the attack and his own whirling emotions. But his sleep wasn't peaceful. His dreams were haunted by the horrors he'd suffered in the last two hundred years.

. . .

The mangled body lay beside him on the ground. He stared at it, horrified. Blood saturated his chest, hands, and face causing him to dry heave several times. The person was beyond unrecognizable. Which villager had he mutilated? Panic and terror caused his body temperature to skyrocket; sweat dripped down his face and built along his skin. The cool early dawn air did nothing to stop the salty slickness drenching him.

How could he live like this? How could he be around his family this way? Oh God! His little sister. His parents. They'd hate him for being a monster. What if he hurt them? Covering his face with his hands, Justin sobbed. He couldn't stay, not when he could end up murdering his family. He struggled to his feet and went to the nearby river to wash the blood away. Light barely tinted the sky as Justin trudged through the forest to his home. No sounds met his ears from inside their cabin, and Justin breathed a small sigh of relief. He couldn't risk seeing them, fearful he would change his mind.

In silence, Justin dressed, his previous clothing having ripped during the change, and packed food and clothing into a satchel he had for collecting herbs for his mother. He wrote a short note telling his family he loved them with all of his heart, but he couldn't stay for fear he'd harm them. Then he snuck back out of the house and went to the barn to saddle his horse. Spartan, an ungelded stallion, snorted and shied away from Justin when he tried to approach. Wildness caused Spartan's eyes to roll, fear-sweat coating his large form. Justin spoke softly, taking precious moments to calm the horse. Eventually he managed to saddle Spartan and swung up into the seat, securing his feet in the stirrups. He urged Spartan through the door, ducking as they passed through, and tapped his heels against Spartan's sides, pushing him to a slight trot.

His heart ached the farther he traveled from the only home he'd ever known. Once he'd gone far enough to where his family wouldn't be able to hear, Justin nudged Spartan into a run and didn't slow him until the horse needed a break. He dismounted and started to walk, leading Spartan behind him. He didn't have a clue how far he made it by the end of the day, but when the sun began to set, the same strange sensations crawled beneath his skin, making him restless and causing Spartan to become skittish again.

He found a place to camp for the night. An itch built inside of him the higher the moon rose, and once at its peak, pain scoured his insides, claws raking at his chest to be free, and Justin screamed in agony. His bones snapped, and Justin writhed on the ground, fire tearing through him. Spartan gave a high pitched whinny and reared upward, trying to break the reins free of the log Justin had tethered him to. Justin had no idea how long it took before he blacked out, but when he woke the next morning, a keening wail left his throat.

Spartan's body lay beside him, mangled almost beyond recognition. Justin gagged and rolled to his hands and knees, vomiting into the grass. Tears streamed down his cheeks at the loss of his best friend. He had no way to bury Spartan and was forced to leave the horse to the wild animals. Guilt and shame raged through him, pushing him onward.

The dream changed, flashing to another event a hundred years later. By then he'd begun hunting others, killing them one by one to try and find the one who'd turned him. He was chasing a werewolf, one he'd sensed close by. His sword gleamed with purpose in the sunlight as he raced down the alley after the creature. Reaching the end, he rounded the corner and struck. Only when the sword embedded into flesh did Justin realize it wasn't the monster he'd expected. He stared in horror as a young girl stepped backward, his sword sliding free from her belly, and she crumpled to the ground. "No!" he screamed.

He knelt beside the girl and gathered her into his arms. Numbness set in as she slowly died in his embrace, her beautiful red hair splayed out across his arm. Her life slipped away while the monster he'd been chasing stood at the end of the alley, laughing maniacally at Justin's mistake. The girl he'd murdered flickered and suddenly Kara lay in his arms. His cries of anguish became howls, his body twisting and cracking, reshaping itself to the monster inside of him. A monster he hated more than anything.

CHAPTER 5

"Justin!" He felt a hand slap his face and a hand on his shoulder, shaking him.

His eyes flew open, and he saw he wasn't in the alley and he hadn't attacked Kara, hadn't killed her. She sat on the edge of the bed in his room. The room in the house they were currently renting. "Kara!"

He sat up and grabbed her to him, tears streaming down his cheeks as he held her. She stroked his hair gently. "Shh. It's just a dream, Justin."

"No, it wasn't," Justin sobbed. "I saw her again, Kara."

Kara knew of his past, knew what he'd done to the young woman and how much he blamed himself. He drew in a ragged breath. His chest felt tight, and a burning sensation settled into his lungs, oxygen not flowing through properly, hindered by his gasps.

"It was an accident, Justin. You didn't mean to kill her, and you've spent every day since trying to avenge her death."

Justin shook his head. "It's not enough. I need to die. Please, Kara, let me die."

Kara's eyes filled with tears at his words, and guilt split Justin's heart even more. He knew Kara loved him, had always loved him, and he knew begging for death would hurt her, but he couldn't bear being a monster any longer. Kara tightened her embrace and fiercely responded, "Never!"

Justin began to calm down, and with a sigh of despair, he said, "I'm sorry, Kara. I know you don't like it when I talk that way. But I see her every single day. I don't know how much more I can stand. In my dreams... she becomes you, and if I ever caused you any harm, I—" He couldn't even finish the sentence as his breath choked in his throat.

"You won't hurt me, Justin," Kara replied with conviction.

"You don't know that. When I become one of them, those monsters, I can't control my actions. If I ever got out of the cage, I wouldn't be able to stop myself," Justin told her angrily.

Kara just held on tighter for a moment without responding and then pulled back. "That guy's here again."

Justin tensed and looked at her. "What?"

"The white-haired guy. The one who kidnapped me."

"Vincent? What the hell is he doing here?" Justin stood and went into his bathroom to wash his face.

"I don't know, but he seemed pretty edgy. I'll go keep him company until you're ready."

He heard the bedroom door snick closed and leaned against the sink, staring at himself in the mirror. A haunted darkness shone from his eyes, and Justin closed them, breathing in deep and letting it out slow and even. He forced away the memories of the girl he'd killed all those years ago. There really was only three nights a month where those green eyes didn't disturb his thoughts.

Justin sighed and pushed away from the sink. He stopped to put on one of his own shirts and picked up Vincent's to return to him. When he entered the kitchen, Vincent had a mug in front of him. Justin laid the shirt on the table by his arm. "Here. Thanks for the loan."

Kara glanced at him with curiosity but didn't ask. He looked away from her and sat across from Vincent. "Why are you here?"

"I spoke to several of the other hunters about what you discovered in the tunnel. In the past there have been whispers of certain spells a werewolf could use in order to choose when they change and to retain control of their bodies when they do. But those were only rumors and conjecture. Until now it seems. Apparently a group of them have located the old scriptures and have learned how to use them."

Justin's gaze shot to Vincent's face in shock. "That's what the chanting was? And that's why they can change in broad daylight?"

"Yes. The others are researching why the werewolves are gathering in groups like the one you encountered. I went back to the alley after you left, but they had already vacated the tunnel."

A spell which could grant them the ability to change at will and to stay aware of who they were? It almost sounded too impossible to believe.

"As much as it pains me to admit it, we need your help." Vincent clenched his teeth hard enough to break them while biting out the sentence, clearly one of the hardest things he'd ever had to admit.

Justin didn't respond immediately. He sat there, lost in thought. Maybe he would finally be able to put the human he'd killed to rest and then himself. Tired of living and tired of searching for the bastard who'd bit him, Justin couldn't imagine a greater peace.

"Well? Are you going to help us or not?" Vincent demanded, sitting straighter in his chair.

Looking at Vincent, Justin replied, "I will. If you'll do one thing for me."

"What?" Vincent asked him, a wary look on his face.

"When it's over, you kill me."

Kara gasped. "No!"

Vincent studied Justin for several silent moments. "All right."

"No, I won't let you! Justin, you can't be serious. Please don't do this," Kara begged.

Justin only gave her a sad glance. "It's a deal then."

A sob came from Kara, but she didn't say another word until they were finished discussing plans and ways they might be able to locate the other werewolves who'd disappeared. Once Vincent left though, Kara lost her control and raged at him. "Why?"

"You know why, Kara. Don't you understand what I go through

every single day? Remembering all of the things I've done? I haven't slept without having nightmares for almost two hundred years."

"Justin, please, don't do this. I-I love you," Kara said, dropping her gaze to her entwined hands.

Justin looked at her with sadness. He cared for her so much, but as a sister, nothing more. "I'm sorry, Kara. I... don't feel the same way. You're like my sister."

"I don't want to be your sister! I want to be with you." Kara threw herself into his arms in desperation and kissed him.

He had no idea what to do except not respond to her passion. She pulled away and looked at him, pain and grief glittering in her eyes. Unable to stand it, he turned his head. "Even if I could feel that kind of love for you, Kara, I'm not free to do so. Don't you understand? If anything happened while we were... together, I could infect you. And I would never be able to forgive myself!"

He stood, forcing her to step back. "I'm going out for a while. I'll be back later."

The sound of Kara sobbing as he tore out of the house broke his heart, and he knew his decision for Vincent to kill him was the best for everyone. Kara would be able to move on, and he wouldn't be a danger to her anymore. He mounted his bike, started the engine, and shot off down the street.

Rain started to fall as Justin drove aimlessly around the city. His hair and clothing were plastered to his skin in moments. The smell of the rain drifted into his nose and triggered a memory of when he'd been a child. He'd been maybe ten years old. His mother and sister were sitting on the front porch, shelling peas, while he helped his father round up the chickens from the yard to bed down for the night. Storm clouds started rolling in, and they were chasing down the last chicken when it started to rain. A big, fat drop had landed on his forehead, and he'd stopped where he stood and let the rain fall on him. He'd breathed in deep the earthy smell, closing his eyes and lifting his face toward the sky. His father had to catch the last chicken and put it in the coop. His mother called to him to get out of the rain, and as he ran toward her with a huge grin on his face, she'd scolded him for getting soaking wet.

His memory twisted, and he tightened his hold on the handlebars of his motorcycle. It was on a night like tonight that he finally met the one who'd bitten him. The silver hair so similar to the bright moonlight haunting Justin and the cocky sneer on the bastard's lips as they'd faced off against each other. Justin hadn't known about the legend then, or he'd have died trying to kill the one who'd turned him. He'd taunted Justin, stunning him long enough to escape. Over the many years since, he'd managed to catch up to him twice more, learning the name to go with the face Justin loathed with every breath—Jake.

It was only thirty years ago when Justin learned of the cure he longed for from another werewolf he'd hunted; they had tried to use it as a bargaining chip for their life, much like Justin was doing with Vincent, he supposed. Yet he'd never gotten close enough to kill Jake since. If he'd known in the beginning and been able to break his curse, maybe he wouldn't have killed so many innocents, and he could have gone home again. The idea of being able to hold his sister once more or to smell the scent of his mother's hair or even see the broad smile on his father's face haunted him.

Tears mingled with the rain now. Painful twinges in his heart caused Justin to gasp for air. He had no particular destination as he drove, but he eventually found himself in front of Vincent's building. He looked up at the apartments and wondered what had brought him there. No lights filtered from the window he figured belonged to Vincent, and Justin knew the hybrid probably was sleeping by then. A noise from his left caught his attention, and Justin glanced over to see a large shadow slipping along the side of the building. Eyes narrowing at the edges, Justin parked his bike and dismounted. He reached down and pulled out the silver knife he kept in his boot and then crept to where the shadow had been. He cursed himself for not ensuring he had his gun back before leaving Vincent's earlier.

Flattening himself against the wall, he peered around the edge and watched as the creature sniffed at the air. When the beast started to turn his way, Justin wrenched backward and waited. A moment later, he leaned toward the edge again, only to find the creature had disappeared. He slipped into the alley and moved down to the back of the apartments, but still nothing. He lifted his head slightly and sniffed at the air. Only a lingering scent of werewolf drifted on the breeze. A low growl rumbled in his chest, and Justin moved away from the building. The slight sound of a pebble shifting above him caught his attention in time to see a large shadow from above aimed right for him.

Justin leapt backwards and felt the ground shake slightly as the creature hit the pavement in front of him. His knife would be useless against the creature. His only chance was to get to Vincent's for a weapon. He dodged around the beast and grabbed onto the fire escape. The rain had made the metal slippery, and he almost lost his grip but managed to hold on by the skin of his teeth. With his inhuman strength, he pulled himself upward and over the first set of steps. His footsteps were loud on the metal, slamming onto each one, fast and hard. He heard the werewolf howl in fury, and it started after him, leaping between the two buildings to catch him, claws digging into the walls to hold on.

Justin reached Vincent's apartment and, looking through the window, saw him asleep on the bed. He opened the window and plunged inside to grab one of the swords resting against the dresser. Not even paying attention to the very much naked Vincent, who'd sat up in bed, he darted back out the window and raced the remainder of the way to the roof. The werewolf howled again and gave chase. Justin sprinted to the other side and launched himself across to the next building. The beast followed, and Justin swung around to face it. "Come on, you ugly bastard! What the hell are you waiting for?" he shouted, brandishing the sword.

Fangs dripping with saliva, the werewolf snarled at Justin, circling around him. Justin struck at the werewolf, but it sidestepped his thrust and swung at him with its giant claws. Justin whirled away from it, and the claws missed by inches. "Justin! Look out!"

Vincent's warning came a second too late, and Justin didn't have time to block a second beast's attack. Razor sharp claws ripped into his side, tearing away part of his flesh. Justin grit his teeth and evaded the next swipe. He saw Vincent gain the attention of the first creature by swinging at it with another sword. The beast howled and turned on Vincent.

Justin and Vincent fought side by side, swords flashing and metal clanging against claws. Vincent managed to slide the tip of his sword into the heart of the werewolf he fought. It let out a roar which no doubt rocked the walls of the building beneath them. The silver had pierced its heart, and seconds later it collapsed, dead.

Vincent moved to assist Justin, but Justin managed to sheath the blade of the sword in the creature's chest. The monster staggered for a moment and then fell forward, grabbing Justin as it fell over the side of the building. Justin closed his eyes at the sensation of free falling. He thought he heard Vincent cry out, but all he could do was try to twist the larger body beneath his. Only he didn't quite succeed, and he hit the ground with half a five-hundred-pound werewolf landing top of him. He grunted and lay there, stunned.

When he finally found the ability to move, he shoved at the werewolf's body, his arms almost buckling from exhaustion, but then the beast began to shift on its own and Justin tensed, wondering if it were still alive. He realized a second later Vincent had hold of the creature and was lifting it off of him.

"Justin," Vincent said with what almost sounded like relief.

Justin snorted in his head as he struggled to his feet. Glaring at the monster, he kicked at it, hard. "Shithead."

"I think we should set that before your bones heal. If we don't it'll heal wrong, and we'll have to break it again."

Justin frowned and looked at his arm. "Oh," he murmured, realizing he must have hit the ground harder than he'd thought. He hadn't even noticed the odd angle the appendage stuck out at. "Yeah."

Vincent took hold of his arm, gentler than Justin would have expected. Justin braced himself against the side of the building. A loud pop crackled in the silence around them when Vincent pulled hard on the limb. Justin clenched his teeth and stifled a scream of agony, tipping his head back onto the brick behind him. "Fuck!"

Blood soaked Justin's shirt yet again, and he sighed, but the large gash in his side should heal soon. He staggered when he tried to straighten away from the wall. "I know it's probably beneath you, but I think I need a little help standing," he said to Vincent weakly.

Even though his werewolf genes made him immortal and hard to kill without beheading or silver, he could still feel pain and could be weakened for an extended period of time. Vincent didn't say anything in response. He stepped closer to Justin's side and slid an arm around his waist. They walked to Vincent's building next door, Justin leaning heavily into Vincent's side. No words were exchanged on the short trip to the building and into the elevator. Only after Vincent helped Justin onto the only chair in his apartment did Vincent break the silence. "I'm going to go take care of the two bodies, and I'll be right back."

Justin nodded and slumped in the chair with his eyes closed. He scented gasoline just before Vincent exited the apartment. He knew the only way to truly dispose of the bodies was to bury them or burn them. He assumed Vincent intended on discarding them in the dumpster behind the building before torching the corpses. Energy completely sapped, Justin found himself drifting into unconsciousness.

CHAPTER 6

Justin didn't know how long he'd been asleep, but the most astonishing part was for the first time in two hundred years he'd slept without dreaming, and when he woke he felt something he hadn't in just as long. Safe. A warm object across his belly registered, and Justin blinked himself awake to find Vincent's arm lying across him. Justin sucked in a sharp breath and turned his head to find Vincent's on the pillow next to him. He studied the strong lines of Vincent's face. Several strands of the shocking white hair lay across his broad forehead. Any model would kill for the perfect line of Vincent's nose, which ended in a pert little upturn. His perusal slid down to the sensual lips. The bottom lip was slightly fuller than the top, and he wanted nothing more than to lean in and feel them both against his own.

What the hell am I thinking? Justin thought to himself. *I need to get the hell out of here.* Just then he felt Vincent's fingers stroke lightly over his skin, and Justin sucked in a breath as arousal shifted through him. Before he could move, to stop the caress sending unwanted heat to his groin, Vincent's eyes opened and stared at him unfocused for several seconds. Then Vincent jolted upright and sat there for a minute, running a hand through his hair. Without a word, Vincent left the bed and went into the adjoining bathroom. Justin stared after him and then heard the shower cut on.

Justin had no intention of being there when Vincent got out of the shower. Those few moments would make everything awkward between them for sure. So Justin got off the bed, borrowed yet another shirt, and left. The night was beginning to fade, the fingers of dawn breaking the inky black sky. Justin started his bike and pulled into the already pretty busy traffic. By the time he got home, Kara had left for work.

He entered the house and went into the kitchen to grab a soda from the fridge. A note sat on the table, and he slid it toward him, uncertain what Kara could have written.

I'm sorry, Justin. I shouldn't have blurted it out like that. Please forgive me. Can we talk tonight when I get home? Love, Kara.

Justin sighed and then headed to his room. He thought back over last night's battle with the werewolves. They were fighting together. Why? When Vincent had yelled to him in warning and he'd seen the other werewolf approaching from behind, he'd been momentarily stunned. Werewolves were solitary beasts. The only thing he could deduce was with the new awareness spell they had discovered they were apparently working toward some common goal or something. But what would they want?

He took a quick shower, dressed, and went back to the kitchen to make some coffee. Even though Kara hated him smoking, he lit a cigarette and sat at the table until the coffee had finished brewing. Just when he'd taken another drag on the cigarette, he heard someone knock on the front door. He debated on ignoring it, but a louder, harder knock came. With a sigh of aggravation, he went to answer it. "Vincent," he said, surprised to see him.

Vincent strode past him into the house without waiting for an invitation. "Sure, just come in," Justin said sarcastically, shutting the door.

"We need to talk about last night."

Justin felt his face heat, a blush spreading over his cheeks, and wondered if something had happened in Vincent's apartment that he didn't remember. "You mean the fight?" he asked.

"Of course I mean the fight. What the hell else would I mean?" Vincent glared at him.

"No-Nothing," Justin stuttered and returned to the kitchen. He grabbed two mugs out of the cabinet near the stove. Along the way he grabbed the cigarette he'd popped into the ashtray.

Vincent abruptly voiced the same thing Justin had been thinking earlier. "You noticed it too, didn't you? They were working together. But why?"

"I don't know. Do you think they're going to try and do something to the humans?" Justin asked, voice muffled slightly with the cigarette perched in the corner of his mouth. He poured coffee in both mugs and set the carafe back down.

"Maybe. I'm more interested in who their alpha is and how they found the spell. According to the archives the hunters have been keeping for the past hundred years, those scrolls were lost several centuries ago."

"Archives?" Justin asked. He set a mug in front of Vincent and sat across from the hybrid to enjoy his own.

"There are more of us, you know," Vincent said, superiority shining through his tone and the cocky tilt of his head. "I'm not the only one. I'm surprised you've managed to avoid hearing about us for so long."

"Yeah, well, I'm not exactly the most sociable being on the planet. I'd heard whispers among the ones I hunted about others, but I didn't care enough to try and find out the truth. We were working toward the same purpose, so I figured if the hunters were real then I was glad to have the help eradicating a species on this earth who cause nothing but death and bloodshed."

"A species to which you belong," Vincent pointed out.

"A species to which I belong, and as soon as this is all over you'll be adding my body to the two you disposed of last night," Justin responded.

A strange look flashed over Vincent's features before he answered. "Fine. Let's start searching for the nest we found the other day. They couldn't have gone far. We'll start at the alley and work out in widening zones until we find them."

They made plans to searching starting that night. There had to be a reason for the attacks and the way the werewolves were no longer trying to hide themselves. Justin decided to bring up what had happened earlier. "Listen, about this morning—"

Vincent interrupted him. "What about this morning? We both needed sleep, and it was the only bed. I move a lot when I sleep. It's nothing, so forget it ever happened." Without another word, he stormed out of the house.

Justin stared after Vincent for several contemplative moments and then went to dress for work. Lee stuck him at the host stand again, and he sighed when he realized his tip monies hadn't been so good lately. Restlessness ate at him while he worked. His skin tingled where Vincent had stroked him, almost as though the touch had been burned into his flesh. He could almost feel the tips of his fingers still touching him. Justin took a short cigarette break in the alley again in the hope Vincent would show, but his shift passed peacefully with no glimpses of the white-haired hybrid.

He used the phone in Lee's office to make a quick call to Kara. She wasn't home yet, so he left a message telling her of his plans to search for the others with Vincent. When he exited the restaurant, he spotted Vincent leaning on the building across the street. He jogged over, dodging through traffic, and stopped beside him.

"I'll head that way." Vincent pointed to the north. "You head that way." He tossed his thumb to the south.

"Fine." Justin started to walk away when Vincent's warm hand landed on his shoulder.

"Watch your ass, wolf," he said.

Justin looked at him in surprise. "Are you worried about me?"

Vincent gave a small snort and replied, "Nah. I just don't want to miss out on the pleasure of killing you myself."

Sighing, Justin headed off the way Vincent had pointed and stopped every so many hundred feet to sniff at the air. He found the scents of food, humans, garbage, and even marijuana, but no wolves. He watched the people walking the streets, looking for any hint one of them wasn't quite human. An itch began in the middle of his shoulder blades, and eventually Justin realized someone followed him. Taking a chance, he glanced over his shoulder, but there were too many people on the sidewalks to tell which one trailed him.

He made a decision to force the person out into the open and turned toward the park where his deal with Vincent began. The crowd began to thin out the closer he got, and the stairs leading into the park were deserted. He stopped at the top and turned. A young blond woman stood at the base of the stairs holding a very deadly-looking crossbow. Justin took a step back as she raised it. He watched her for a split second longer and then realized where he'd seen her before. She'd been the woman with Vincent in the restaurant the first day they'd met. *Son of a bitch. He sent her to kill me.*

Without waiting any further, he turned and sprinted across the park. An arrow whipped by his head and thwacked into a tree inches from hitting him instead. *Shit, she really intends to kill me!* His feet slapped against the ground as he bolted with preternatural speed to the other side of the park. Crashing through the bushes, he raced into the street, narrowly missing being hit by a car. The lights of the vehicle blinded him momentarily, and that hesitation cost him dearly. An arrow bit into his shoulder, and the pain struck him hard. Worse than even breaking his arm. The arrows were silver-tipped, and the silver began eating away at his flesh instantly.

He grabbed the arrow and tried to remove it while running, but only succeeded in snapping the arrow off, leaving the tip still buried in his shoulder. The wound couldn't heal itself with the silver in it, which caused blood to pour down his arm. Droplets littered the ground like paint from a brush being flung haphazardly. The blond began to gain on him, and he wondered if he were finally at the end. Was this how he'd go out?

When he darted between two buildings, another arrow just missed his head, embedding into the building to his right, and he winced. His only regret would be not getting the chance to say goodbye to Kara. Then Vincent's face flashed before his eyes, and he almost stopped running. Why the hell would he think of the hybrid when the whole reason he ran for his life was Vincent?

Finally, he reached the restaurant he worked at and turned into the alley behind it. Unfortunately, the back door had been locked for the first time in forever during business hours. Now he'd trapped himself with nowhere to go. He swung around to face her. She stood at the end of the alley, her crossbow trained on him. "What? Vincent too afraid to take me on himself? Or is it too distasteful to betray me after our deal?"

The blond sneered and said, "Vincent's getting soft. Letting a monster run around the city without putting it down. I knew what you were. Vincent was supposed to take care of you. Then I find out he's actually *working* with you."

Justin's eyes widened in surprise. Vincent hadn't sent the girl. He saw her finger tighten on the trigger and braced himself for the blow. "I saw you last night," she said, disgust evident in her tone.

"Saw me?" he asked.

"Through the window, lying in bed with him. You've poisoned him. Bewitched him with some kind of magic. A month ago, he would have killed you as soon as look at you. Now I see him, *sleeping* with a monster. It's repulsive." Anger radiated from her. "I'm going to kill you to help him break free of your curse."

Just as the arrow released, a dark form hurled itself at her and knocked her to the ground. The arrow came straight at Justin, and he attempted to dodge it, but the silver already streaming through his veins caused his movements to be impeded. He hissed when it nicked his already wounded shoulder.

"What the hell are you doing, Yasmine?" Vincent demanded, picking her up off the ground.

Justin stood there watching them argue while gripping his shoulder, hoping to stem the flow of blood.

"You've lost your mind, Vincent! How can you possibly be working with a werewolf?" Yasmine demanded.

"Because he wants those monsters dead just as much as I do, if not more!" Vincent shouted in her face.

"He's poisoned your mind! You can't possibly believe he wants to kill his own kind, do you?"

"I've seen him do it, Yasmine. You have no right to interfere here. I didn't ask for your help," he growled at her.

Justin staggered and slumped into the side of the building. The silver weakened him further the longer it remained in his body. Vincent hurried to his side, sliding an arm around Justin's waist and lifting his good arm around his shoulders.

"Those were silver tipped arrows, and they were dipped in silver nitrate. He's going to have a very painful night, *if* he survives. I could put him down. Speaking humanely, of course."

Vincent glared at Yasmine, supporting Justin's entire weight. "Go home. If you try to kill him again, I'll be there to put you down first!"

Yasmine reared back in shock. "You'd kill a hunter? You really have been poisoned. Wait until the others hear about this. They'll hunt you down, too."

"They know about him. I've already contacted the others. Now go home!"

Yasmine stared for a charged minute and then turned and disappeared without another word. Vincent pulled Justin tighter to him and started walking. "I'm always saving your ass, wolf."

Justin laughed weakly. "I guess so."

"It's amazing you've survived as long as you have. You must have been flying on sheer dumb luck. We need to get that arrow out and get sodium chloride into your bloodstream. It's the only way to combat the nitrate," Vincent explained.

Groaning, Justin knew Yasmine's words were no lie. He was in for a very painful night.

CHAPTER 7

By the time they made it back to Vincent's, he could barely hold onto Vincent or walk. His veins were on fire. A million flames licked along his body, and he started to shake. Vincent picked him up and carried him the remainder of the way to his apartment, kicking the door open and then shut again.

He laid Justin on the bed and ripped the shirt from around the protruding arrow. "I'm beginning to think you like ripping the clothes off me," Justin joked breathlessly.

Vincent didn't say anything. He grabbed a sharp dagger from a drawer by his bed and looked at him. "This is going to hurt."

"Yeah, no shit." Justin stifled a scream when the dagger dug into his shoulder. He felt the metal against metal as the knife pulled at the tip of the arrow.

His vision began to blur from the pain. What felt like hours later, the silver tip slid free from his shoulder, and Vincent tossed it onto the nightstand. Vincent grabbed a container from the fridge, and Justin groaned when he knew what was coming. "You keep a supply of that in your fridge?" Justin asked.

"I may be a hybrid, but we still suffer from some of the same weaknesses you werewolves do. You might want to put this in your mouth."

He handed Justin a smooth wooden stick, about an inch and a half thick.

Justin took the stick from him and slipped it between his teeth. Vincent climbed onto the bed and placed one knee on Justin's chest. He opened the container of common table salt and, with a grimace, dumped about a cup of salt into the wound. When the salt hit the shredded flesh, Justin cried out and bit down on the stick, almost cracking it in half. Agony caused his body to jerk upward, and he would have come straight off the bed if not for Vincent's knee. But when Vincent began to grind the salt into the wound, his teeth finished off breaking the stick in two. His mind, unable to take anymore, blessedly shut down, and he lost consciousness.

～

Seeing Justin's body go lax all of a sudden sent panic flowing through Vincent, and he reached out to check for a pulse. The steady, if fast, pulse beneath his fingers caused him to huff a sigh of relief, one he wouldn't analyze because he should be ecstatic another monster had been wiped off the planet. He removed the pieces of wood from Justin's mouth, ensuring there were no splinters remaining, and got up to return the salt to his fridge.

Another sigh erupted from his mouth when he looked back at Justin lying in his bed. This was beginning to become a habit. Moving over to Justin's side, Vincent carefully removed his boots and dropped them near the chair Justin had sat in just hours ago, then covered Justin with a blanket. He threw the silver arrowhead into the trash, then washed the dagger and placed it in the nightstand drawer. After he finished cleaning everything, he grabbed a couple of blankets from the small closet and made himself a bed on the floor. He wouldn't share the bed with Justin again, not when Yasmine's words replayed in his head. He'd been hidden in the shadows nearby while she'd yelled at Justin. The implication behind her words had been clear. She'd assumed they'd had sex.

A shiver raced through his body at the thought, and he rolled over, shutting that shit down. No way would he even think of having sex with a monster. But the idea kept creeping through. Justin wasn't exactly hard on the eyes. His lean muscular frame, though a bit smaller than his own, could tempt anyone, even a saint. The shoulder-length dark hair made Vincent think of those nights when no moon shone overhead; the inky blackness was broken up by his eerily light blue eyes. Those eyes were more expressive than Justin even realized. Vincent could tell Justin found him attractive. Desire seemed to darken the light color to a turquoise.

Sliding both hands beneath his head as a pillow, Vincent stared at the ceiling while listening to Justin's steady breathing. He didn't want to admit his own lust for Justin because, despite how much and how hard he denied it to himself, he did desire to taste Justin. Would his lips be soft or firm beneath his? Over the centuries he'd been alive, Vincent had indulged in sexual encounters with men and women, never staying in one place long enough to grow attached. Somehow Justin had managed to do what none of those others had… he'd gotten under Vincent's skin.

He thought back to the first time he'd seen Justin in the alley behind the restaurant. Even though he'd known the boy was a werewolf, he'd still felt his body react to the sexy way Justin moved, the small stud in his ear glinting in the light when he turned his head, and the full lips wrapped around the filter of a cigarette. Vincent scowled at the dark ceiling. What the hell was wrong with him? When had he turned soft? Rolling to his stomach, he buried his face in his arms and, just before drifting off to sleep, he swore to himself he'd kill Justin when their truce ended.

Justin jerked awake, confused about where he was, but everything began to slowly come back to him. Once again he found himself in Vincent's bed in his apartment. His shoulder didn't hurt, and he no longer felt the fire licking along his veins. Weakness still caused his muscles to quiver, and his hand shook when he raised it to rake his fingers through his hair to straighten the mess. The effects of the silver nitrate would take several more hours to fully disappear. He fell back onto the mattress and started to pick apart the events from the previous evening. Yasmine, another hunter, had been angry, very angry, about Vincent working with him.

Justin had seen the hurt in her eyes when she'd spit venom about the two of them in bed together. Did she love Vincent? But Vincent didn't seem to care for her. The way Vincent had spoken to her and defended him surprised Justin. He remembered the malice in her dark brown eyes. She wanted him dead. Vincent's parting words to the woman resounded in his head. *If you try to kill him again, I'll be there to put you down first.* The idea Vincent would kill a hunter to keep her from killing him caused a strange feeling in his chest. One he didn't want to spend much time thinking about.

A small noise came from the floor beside the bed, and Justin rolled to the edge to look down at Vincent. Vincent slept on his stomach, face buried in his arms. A soft moan came from Vincent, and Justin wondered what the hybrid dreamed about. Vincent flipped onto his back, and Justin jerked away in shock when Vincent whispered something which sounded suspiciously like his name.

Justin shook his head. Vincent must have been dreaming of killing him. The idea of anything else tripped Justin's weirded out switch. He spotted his boots and carefully eased off the bed. Stuffing his feet into them, Justin figured his shirt was intact enough to make it home without drawing attention to himself, though the late hour would help. Crossing to the window, he opened it and sat down on the ledge. Easing his body sideways, he slid one leg out and then the other, but the sound of a harsh, "What are you doing?", came from the darkness behind him, forcing him to freeze partway through.

Turning his head, Justin could see Vincent sitting up with a pissed off expression. "What?" he asked, brows furrowing in confusion.

"You shouldn't be moving, you idiot."

"Why? What's wrong with me moving?"

"Moving too soon before your body has the chance to filter out all of the silver nitrate can cause it to speed through you even faster. It's a ticking time bomb. Even with the salt in your veins, it takes a while for it to eat away at all of it."

"I'm fine. I need to get home. Kara is going to be worried."

Vincent growled and, within a blink of an eye, stood next to him and yanked him back through the window. He tossed Justin on the bed as if he weighed nothing. Justin hadn't expected the actions and lay there, dumbfounded. In a move which stunned Justin even more, Vincent straddled him, holding him down, his wrists pressed into the bed by Vincent's hands. He opened his mouth to ask what the hell Vincent thought he was doing, but he stopped any words Justin may have uttered by slamming his mouth onto of his.

A warm, wet tongue thrust deep into Justin's mouth, and Justin lost all coherent thought, a moan rattling in his throat. He desperately returned the kiss, carding his fingers through the long white hair and tugging Vincent down to cover him completely. Vincent groaned when his body met Justin's hard length. Their hands were everywhere, exploring anything they could reach. Vincent slipped his leg between Justin's, pushing against the aching flesh pulsing under Justin's pants. Justin gasped into Vincent's mouth and rocked his hips, grinding along the bulging muscle of Vincent's thigh.

Justin released a guttural cry when Vincent cupped his cock through his jeans and squeezed gently. Then suddenly Vincent was gone. Panting, Justin tried to wrap his head around what had happened, his cock about ready to burst out of his jeans. Vincent stood there, chest heaving, a strange expression on his face. Both their breathing sounded loud in the silence.

Vincent's sudden movement of grabbing his trench coat and slamming out of the apartment caused Justin to flinch. The abrupt exit left Justin even more confused. Justin stood from the bed, and to avoid any chance of running into Vincent, left through the still open window. He bolted along the sidewalk and mentally berated himself for allowing what happened in Vincent's bedroom. *What the hell was that?*

He reached the house he shared with Kara in under an hour, his supernatural abilities giving him the extra burst of speed. Opening the front door with his key, Justin itched for a cigarette. Smoking helped him process, or at least he felt like it did. He shut the door quietly, knowing he didn't want to wake Kara. He entered the kitchen and dug out a pack of cigarettes he'd buried in the cabinet with their canned goods. The scent of the cigarette hit his nostrils, and Justin almost groaned as he slid the filtered end between his lips and grabbed the lighter on the counter. The flint flicked several times before lighting, and the first draw into his lungs caused Justin to feel lightheaded.

He set coffee to brew and plopped down into a chair at the table. Smoke drifted into the air from the cigarette as he watched the end burn. Justin set it in the ashtray and propped his elbows on the table, dropping his face into his hands. The soft sound of footsteps brought his head up. Kara stood in the doorway in a robe with a sad expression. He tried to smile, but it fell flat. She came further into the room and took the chair across from him. They didn't speak for several long moments, and the silence was rather loud around them.

Finally, Kara rubbed at her eyes, then said, "I'm sorry, Justin. I didn't mean to push you like that. I-I understand you don't feel the same way about me, but please don't keep me out of your life."

"I do love you, Kara, just… not like that. I'm not keeping you out of my life. I'm sorry I've been absent so much the last two days. The werewolves have been working together. Something we could never anticipate. Vincent and I have been searching for them." Justin went on to tell her about the nest, the spell, the other hunters, the archives, and Yasmine. He avoided the moment in Vincent's bed.

"She tried to kill you?" Kara asked, horrified.

"And would have succeeded if not for Vincent. He actually saved me." Justin gave a humorless laugh. "To think a hunter actually saved a werewolf, or that he threatened one of his own if they tried to hurt me again."

Kara studied him, speculation in her eyes. "Did something happen, Justin?"

"What do you mean?"

"You seem different. Sadder than usual."

She knew him too well. He couldn't tell her about the hot but brief make out session in Vincent's bed or the loss he'd felt when Vincent broke it off. "Nothing happened, Kar. I'm just tired."

He didn't wait for her to press the subject and left the kitchen.

CHAPTER 8

The next day, Justin did something he hadn't done in a long time—he called out sick from work for a few days. He wrote a note for Kara, telling her he needed some time away, but he would be back. He assured her it had nothing to do with her, and he told her he loved her. Justin threw some clothing and money into a bag, strapped his sword to his back, and took off out of the house. His bike had been left at the restaurant, so he made a quick trip there to retrieve it. The wind pulled at his hair and clothes, and he pushed the motorcycle faster.

He drove aimlessly for a couple hours before he pulled over to the side of the road. There was a beautiful lake off to the left of the road, and he walked down the hill to stand at the edge of it. A handful of boats glided over the smooth surface of the water. So many things had happened in the last two weeks; meeting Vincent, almost being killed, Kara's confession, his pact with the hunter, and the stolen moments in Vincent's apartment. All of it overwhelmed him to where he could barely breathe. He just needed time away from everything, time to think if he'd made the right choices.

They'd also had no luck in finding the one who'd bitten him. He had no idea if they ever would, and the idea of Vincent putting him down seemed the more likely chance of making things right. Justin picked up a flat stone nearby, pulled his arm back, and flung it. As he watched it bounce over the water, he knew his days were numbered, and for some reason, it saddened him how he'd never see Vincent's face after that.

He walked back to his bike and climbed on, deciding to keep moving. Maybe he could outrun his reality. His ass had gone numb by mid-afternoon, and the next town he came upon he figured would be a good place to plant himself for a few days. He stopped a couple on the sidewalk to ask for directions to a cheap motel. They pointed him to a nearby three-story building, and Justin thanked them with a nod and smile.

Half an hour later, he found himself ensconced in a small room, but a bed and bathroom were all he needed. Justin dropped his bag by the door and sat down to pull off his boots before flopping back onto the bed. A sigh huffed out of him, and he rolled to his side, curling up into a half fetal position. The idea of going back to face Kara, Vincent, and whatever was left of his lifespan settled like a rock in his stomach. He couldn't even be sure he'd have the strength to return to Tokyo after this. He wished Yasmine had succeeded in her quest to kill him. At least then he couldn't have caused Kara any further pain or burdened Vincent any longer.

The thoughts chased each other around in his brain similar to a toy train, a never ending circle of self-loathing and depression. Justin growled in frustration and grabbed one of the pillows, shoving it over his head, but the plush object couldn't keep them out. He closed his eyes tight and prayed for sleep, yet even then he knew he'd never escape the memories.

~

Vincent managed only a couple hours of sleep before giving up the fight and getting dressed. He got into his car and found himself in front of where Justin worked. For several long minutes, he found himself sitting there, engine off, staring at the front of the restaurant. What the hell was he doing? Why couldn't he get Justin out of his mind? His thoughts drifted to the memory of the heated moments in his bed, and Vincent slammed his palm against the steering wheel. Heat filled his loins, and his lips were desperate for another taste of Justin. Never in his life had he felt this kind of attraction for anyone. There had to be something Justin had done to him. Right? How else could he possibly want the man who turned into a mindless monster three nights a month?

Scowling, he exited his car and entered the restaurant. He needed answers from Justin on just what the hell he had done to him. Only, his angry bubble was popped when the hostess told him Justin had called out sick for a few days. He grunted at her and then spun on his heels, slamming through the front door back onto the sidewalk. He didn't get more than two steps before Kara stood in his way, rage and hatred shining at him. "What do you want?" he snapped.

"What the hell did you do to him?" she demanded.

"What? I didn't do anything to him," he replied defensively. "Why? What are you talking about?"

"He left," she snarled, shoving a piece of paper in his face.

He took the paper from her, opened it, and read the words Justin had written. Vincent closed his eyes for a split second, unwilling to show Kara how much Justin's disappearance affected him. When he opened them, he sneered at her. "So, he decided to run away, did he? Thinks he'll get out of our deal this way?"

Maybe he hadn't expected it or maybe he'd figured he'd deserved it, but his head jerked to the right when her palm connected with his cheek. "You son of a bitch," she growled. "Stay the fuck away from him. Do you hear me? Just go back to wherever the hell you came from."

Vincent reached up to touch his smarting cheek while she stomped away. Justin didn't seem the type to run from a problem, not with how he rushed headlong into anything he did without fear of being hurt or killed. So why did Justin leave? The note said Justin would return, but a feeling of dread filled his belly and something akin to fear joined it. A fear Vincent refused to admit. One of Justin not coming back.

Swearing under his breath, Vincent stalked to his car and figured his time would best be spent searching for the group of werewolves.

$\sim$

Justin managed to sleep through until the next morning, but not without dreaming, plagued by the past horrors he always dreamed of interspersed with flashes of a certain hybrid with violet eyes. To distract himself from emotions he couldn't separate, he decided to explore the town he'd stopped in. There were several small shops and even a market place.

He found a beautiful silver necklace he knew Kara would love. Even though money was tight, he bought it anyway. He knew it wouldn't begin to make up for everything he'd put her through these last ten years. Sometimes he wished he had ended up in someone else's yard that day so she would never have become involved in the nightmare of his life. Yet if he'd never met her his life would be intrinsically different, and he may even have ended up hurting more innocent people.

A pair of deep purple amethyst studs caught Justin's eye, and his hand hovered over them, a war raging inside of him. He fingered one of them, watching the stone flash in the light. Vincent roused more than anger and irritation. Especially after the kiss they'd shared. Giving into the urge in his belly, Justin bought them, all the while wondering if the hunter would like them. Would Vincent even accept them?

He continued browsing the various shops but didn't buy anything else, instead choosing to stop for a coffee and a snack at a nearby café. He entered and walked up to the counter, looking over the various images of drinks and food. After placing his order, he wandered to a free table on the sidewalk outside and sat down. The scent of one of his kind drifted on the breeze, and Justin tensed, glancing around without making it obvious. A tall, husky man opened the door of a bakery across the street and entered. Justin strolled over and pretended to study the menu on a sign outside the bakery while watching the man walk toward the back of the shop.

Another distinct scent of werewolf slammed into Justin. His heart raced when he realized a couple drifted into the bakery and followed the other to the back. Justin wondered if somehow he'd been lucky enough to stumble on the new location of the wolves from Tokyo. He settled in and watched them come and go over the next two days, changing his locale from the café to the nearby rooftops. He counted a minimum of twenty different werewolves, but there could be even more for all he knew.

They were always in human form, no indication of changing, but Justin supposed it would be stupid to do that in broad daylight around the humans. Late the second night of his stakeout, he stood atop the roof of the building across from the bakery. There was a steady stream of them entering, and they seemed in a hurry. Uneasiness settled into his stomach at how they were working together. It just didn't fit the usual habits of the monsters he'd learned so much about. They were solitary creatures, preferring to stay away from one another.

Justin, so intent on the activity at the bakery, didn't notice the beast making its way up the side of the building he crouched on. The sky held no light, the moon buried in the shadow of the earth. A scraping of nails on the asphalt of the roof was the only warning he had before the werewolf charged him. He barely managed to pull his sword and the beast was on him. Justin swung the sword upward, catching the werewolf on the claw. The beast roared and slashed at Justin again.

He sliced the werewolf's arm open, blood splattering across Justin's cheek. A howl of pain and fury ripped through the air, and Justin knew at this rate they would attract the others. So in a dance of slash and retreat, Justin led it across to the next roof and then the next. He vaulted to the final building in the row of them, and he turned to face off with the creature once more. It approached him at a fast clip, saliva dripping from its massive fangs, claws furled at the ready.

Justin leapt out of the way on its first swipe and struck back, missing by a hairsbreadth. The beast scrambled around and rushed at him again. He evaded the attack and countered with his own. This time his sword made contact with the creature's chest, slamming through the ribcage to the heart. A shriek loud enough to almost shatter Justin's eardrums pierced the night air as the silver invaded the werewolf's body. Justin yanked his sword free, and the beast crashed to the roof top. He watched without remorse while the werewolf took its last breath, and he wondered about his own upcoming demise. Would he look so pitiful?

He couldn't finish this alone. He knew he needed to call Vincent and alert him to the discovered location and the number of wolves gathering. Disposing of the beast's body would have to wait.

Returning to the hotel, Justin snatched up the phone and dialed Kara's as he had no clue of Vincent's. A couple of rings and then he heard, "Hello?"

Just the sound of her voice eased some of the loneliness in his heart. "Kara. It's me."

"Justin! Where are you? Please come home. I miss you," Kara begged.

"I can't right now, Kara. There's something going on here, and I need you to do me a favor."

"All right. What do you need me to do?"

"Get Vincent and—"

She cut him off. "Vincent! Why? He's done nothing but cause problems since you met him. I know he's the reason you left," Kara accused.

"Kara, I can't explain it right now. I just need you to get Vincent. Tell him he needs to get here. *Now!*" He gave her directions to Vincent's place and then to the hotel he was at.

"I don't like this, but I'll do it. Please be careful."

A loud crash brought Justin spinning around, and he dropped the phone. He heard Kara's voice shouting through the phone as he dove for his sword, too late. Three large men swarmed the room, the door splintered into pieces. One of them transformed right there, shredding its clothing. Justin tried to fight them off, but the one who'd shifted picked him up by the throat and tossed him across the room. He grunted as his body slammed into the television atop the dresser, the screen shattering and plaster from the wall behind it raining down on him. His head struck the corner of the dresser as he fell, knocking him unconscious. The last thing he saw was the two still human men rushing to grab him. As darkness sucked him under, Justin knew he wouldn't be able to keep his end of the bargain with Vincent.

CHAPTER 9

Vincent woke to the sound of someone pounding on his front door. He sat up and raked a hand through his hair, shaking it out, before he climbed from the bed to answer it. The red-headed feisty woman who'd slapped him only a matter of days ago barged into his apartment. "Justin needs your help," she snarled.

He blinked at her, still hazy from disrupted sleep. "What?"

"I said, Justin needs your help!" Kara rounded on him, hands on her hips. "Please, you have to help him!"

"Tell me what's going on first, and then I'll tell you if I'm going to help him."

A sliver of fear for Justin trickled through him when she described the conversation she'd had with him and the loud crashing noise in the background. He rubbed at his bare chest, right over his heart. Did he actually care for Justin?

Halfway through Kara's story, he started dressing. He pulled on a pair of tight black jeans and a sleeveless t-shirt with a faded logo of some band on it. She'd finished by the time he'd slid into his combat boots and laced them up. Everything she'd relayed worried him, but the fact she'd heard an obvious attack happening before the phone went dead scared the hell out of him.

"You're going to help him?" she asked.

Vincent grabbed a duffle bag and started filling it with guns, silver bullets, a couple of small crossbows, silver tipped arrows, and a change of clothing. "I'm going to stop the werewolves. Helping Justin is merely part of a common goal we share."

He hefted the bag off the bed, snatched up the two silver swords, and wrenched open his door.

"Wait!" she called to him.

He stopped and looked at her impatiently. The need to find Justin and ensure no harm had come to the werewolf rode him hard. "What?"

"No matter why you're helping him… Thank you." With that simple statement, she brushed past him and left.

Vincent didn't waste another second, heading to the parking garage and the sleek black Dodge Challenger waiting for him. He tossed his weapons in the trunk and climbed in. The engine started with a deep growl, echoing off the cement pillars. In minutes he'd exited the garage and was on his way out of the city. Out on the empty open road, he pushed the gas, and the needle edged closer to a hundred with each increasing mile. He prayed he wasn't too late.

With purpose in mind, it only took a couple of hours to reach the address Kara had given him. The sun hadn't risen just yet, and the hotel residents appeared to still be slumbering; even the desk clerk had nodded off at the front. Vincent didn't see any evidence of police having been called in, and he grimaced at the idea the wolves had gotten hold of other spells, like the ones the hunters used to hide the fighting and killing they did. It was the only thing that made sense if the humans hadn't heard the ruckus Kara had described.

The moment he stepped out of the elevator on the third floor, the stench of wolf assaulted his nostrils and he growled, jaw clenched tight. There were three distinct scents. No way Justin could have taken on all three. He prayed he wouldn't find Justin dead when he reached the room with the blown out door.

Pulling his sword, he entered the room. The phone lay buzzing with an annoying busy signal on the nightstand. The mattress lay half off the box spring. Vincent swallowed when he saw a backpack lying next to the dresser, some clothing hanging half out of the top. He checked the bathroom, but no Justin. He didn't analyze the relief in his belly. On the way out, he noticed something sparkling on the carpet. He frowned and picked up the silver objects, finding them to be silver earring studs with amethyst stones and a necklace with a moon and star dangling at the end. Had one of the wolves dropped them? Maybe they were Justin's? Vincent shoved them in his pocket and snatched up the backpack.

That's when he noticed Justin's sword sitting in the debris of what looked to once be a television. Blood on the corner of the dresser caught his eye, and Vincent swore underneath his breath. He made sure there was nothing of Justin's remaining before he left, ensuring no one saw him exit the destroyed hotel room.

He headed to the address of the bakery, which was only a few blocks from the hotel. A couple of buildings down, he pulled the Challenger into an alley and shut off the engine. Getting out, he sniffed at the air, but didn't catch the scent of any werewolves. He strapped on his swords, shoved one gun into his waistband and another into his boot. Nothing remarkable stood out about the bakery. Justin had to be mistaken about the number of wolves he'd seen. There couldn't possibly be so many in such a small building.

Was there a tunnel beneath the bakery maybe? Vincent figured the best way to get in would be around back. He moved swiftly down the alley and around to the rear of the building. Nothing unusual there either. The door was locked, of course, and he had to turn it hard, breaking the knob. He quietly entered to find a typical kitchen with several ovens, island tables with muffin tins and bread pans on them, and multiple counters holding big tubs of flour and sugar. Again, nothing looked unusual or out of place.

A sound to his left brought him to a crouch to blend into the shadows behind one of the islands. Someone entered the kitchen. From the smell Vincent could tell they were a werewolf. Vincent peered around the counter and watched when the creature, in human form, headed straight to a freezer in the corner of the room. It opened the huge metal door and walked inside.

Eyes widening, Vincent crept over to the freezer and opened it carefully in case the beast waited on the other side. When he looked in, he saw a set of stairs leading into a dark tunnel. *Slick bastards*, he thought to himself as he silently, but swiftly, made his way down the stairs. His enhanced eyesight as a hybrid allowed him to see in the dark without needing a flashlight. Low murmurs reached his ears, getting louder the further into the tunnel he went. He realized they were chanting. A light began to seep through the darkness, and Vincent pressed himself against the wall, his coat protecting his back from the rough bricks.

When he reached the entrance to the room where he could hear the chanting, he stopped and risked a quick look around the doorframe. His heart pounded when he realized there were at least a hundred wolves in the room. All of them were in human form and kneeling before a large pedestal, where a man stood with a scroll in his hand. Vincent narrowed his gaze when he realized the scroll must contain the spell the archives spoke of.

The man holding the parchment appeared to be in his early twenties, but Vincent knew the looks to be deceptive, as wolves don't age once they're infected. Silver hair hung down into his eyes as the man read aloud with the others. Blue jeans, faded and ripped, hugged the long, thick length of his legs, while a tight black t-shirt clung to his muscular torso. Vincent had no idea how the others could possibly follow someone who looked to be still in high school.

Vincent's gaze flitted away from the apparent leader to land on Justin. He barely stifled the growl in his throat. Justin hung, unconscious, chained to the wall. Naked from the waist up, Justin had trails of blood dripping down his chest, thin lines obviously created by a whip. Vincent had to get a tight grip on himself to keep from rushing in and getting them both killed. At least Justin was alive.

Being careful not to draw attention to himself, he turned and retreated back down the tunnel. He needed to get the rest of the hunters or else Justin would die. Thankfully he made it out of the bakery and back to his car without running into any others. He grabbed his cell and hit Yasmine's name in his contact list. The sky began to lighten, and Vincent knew he couldn't leave the car where he was. It would draw too much attention. So he moved to the alley behind the bakery, but parked two doors down. He prayed Yasmine would answer. The first call went to voice mail, and he tried again.

Finally, she answered. "What do you want, Vincent?"

If he cared, he may have been regretful of how their last encounter went with how cold she sounded, but he had meant every word he'd said to her. He quickly explained about the nest of wolves and the scroll. "I can't stop them all myself. I need the rest of the hunters here, as fast as they can gather."

"I thought you had the *wolf* to help you. Why do you need the hunters?"

"Yasmine, enough. You know how I feel, and it won't change. Are you trying to piss me off?" he demanded.

Yasmine remained silent for the span of a few breaths and then replied, "I'll make the calls."

She hung up. A plan had been put into place where one hunter would call three and those three would call another three until all of the hunters were alerted to the need for help. Vincent made the other two calls he needed and then tossed the phone in the console. He dropped his head into his hands and tried to find the calmness he usually felt. The memory of the whip marks on Justin's skin brought a growl erupting forth. Vincent would gut the fucker who'd tortured Justin.

Thinking that way caused Vincent to squirm in his seat, his hands moving to grip the steering wheel. He knew his feelings toward Justin were irrational at best. After all, how could he possibly care about one of the monsters he'd spent his entire life hunting? Yet Vincent knew somehow Justin had evoked something inside of him he'd never encountered in his past. A longing for something more.

Movement disrupted Vincent's musings, and he saw two of the beasts leave by the back door. He saw another three after them. He began to count, tracking how many exited the building. By noon, he'd seen almost every werewolf who'd been in the ritual room depart. The only one he hadn't witnessed had been the leader at the pedestal, but he'd take his chances. Sliding out of his car, he stuck close to the building, carrying one sword in his hand with the other strapped to his back. He couldn't leave Justin there.

The back door lock hadn't been repaired, and Vincent snuck in, quickly making his way over to the metal door. He kept his footsteps quiet until he reached the room. Vincent halted and peered around the doorway. Justin still hung from chains against the wall, but he was now awake and glaring at the obvious leader. "Kill me and get it over with, Jake," Justin demanded.

Jake tipped his head to the side and smirked. "But I'm having so much fun. You know, at first, I found you rather annoying when you started pursuing me all those years ago. Now, it's just amusing how desperate you are to become a weak little human again." Leaning forward, Jake used his tongue to trace a trail of blood up along the skin of Justin's chest. "You taste good. I might just keep you for a bit. It's been a while since I've had a toy to amuse myself with. In fact, you might find you'll begin to like it."

Vincent growled low in his throat at the sight of the bastard touching what was his. He stepped out of the shadows and into the room. "Get your filthy fucking hands off of him."

Jake whipped around in surprise and then sneered at Vincent. "Jealous are we, hunter? Isn't this sweet? After all these years, you've found yourself a protector, Justin, and a hunter at that! To think I was beginning to believe you might actually kill yourself."

CHAPTER 10

Relief flooded Justin when Vincent appeared in the doorway. "Vincent," he whispered.

He had eyes for nothing except Vincent. His heart beat fierce, ready to burst from his chest.

"You'd better prepare yourself, hunter, because you're going to die," Jake snarled.

Justin watched Vincent transfer the sword in his right hand to his left and then pull a second sword from a sheath on his back. Jake laughed. "You don't think those two little pieces of metal are going to hurt me, do you?"

Jake's voice distorted on the last of his words as he began to shift. His body reshaped and lengthened. The sound of bones cracking and reconnecting echoed in the empty ritual room. In seconds, the beast towered over Vincent by at least a foot and a half. Jake roared and swiped at Vincent. Vincent used one sword to block the attack and swung with the other, attempting to catch Jake off guard, but Jake deflected Vincent's move in time.

Justin could do nothing but watch the two fight ferociously. Metal clanged against claws. He pulled at the chains, trying to free them from the wall, but all he managed to do was rub his wrists raw. His strength had been sapped from him by the beatings Jake had given him and the loss of blood.

Vincent thrust one of the swords deep into Jake's belly, and Justin stared in shock when Jake roared in pain and dropped to his knees. The silver caused enough debilitating pain to give Vincent time to free Justin. The chains rattled against the wall as Vincent caught Justin, wrapped a strong arm around his waist, and slid Justin's arm around his shoulders. He supported Justin through the tunnel and out onto the street behind the bakery.

The brightness of the sun after hours of being locked in darkness and low candlelight stung his eyes. He squeezed them shut while Vincent helped him into a vehicle close to the building. Exhaustion sank deep into Justin's bones, and he barely registered Vincent tossing his swords in the backseat or climbing into the driver's side. The engine gave a low snarl, and then they were roaring out of there.

Justin lay his head back on the seat and concentrated on breathing. He felt a little giddy Vincent had actually come to save him. He'd almost lost hope as the hours slipped away. After all, the werewolves would accomplish what Vincent intended all along, so why bother to worry about getting there in time to help him?

Justin remembered being on the phone with Kara and explaining everything to relay to Vincent when they came crashing into his hotel room. They'd managed to knock him unconscious, and when he'd woken, he'd found himself in a huge room, with no windows and only a single door. He'd been chained to a wall. As he struggled to get loose, he'd heard, "It won't work, Justin."

He'd been horrified to see the one werewolf he'd been chasing for almost two hundred years. "Ah, I so love to see that expression on your face. It turns me on." Jake approached him and slid one hand over Justin's abdomen and along his pec.

"Don't touch me!" Justin spat, yanking at the chains in a desperate desire to get away from the touch causing bile to rise in his throat.

"Now, now, Justin. You shouldn't insult the one who has you in chains. It only makes them angry." His fingernails lengthened slightly, and he trailed one tip across his skin. A thin line of blood appeared, and Justin flinched in pain.

"Such beauty." Jake traced the line with his tongue, lapping at the blood. He stepped away and retrieved a wicked-looking whip from the pedestal nearby. The crack as he swung it into the empty air close to Justin's cheek sent a shiver of terror down Justin's spine. "I'm going to make you an offer you would be wise to accept, pup. I heard you're working with the hybrid. If you join with us, help us kill him, I'll let you live. If you refuse, I'll do so many wonderfully painful things to your body you'll wish I'd finished what I started two hundred years ago."

Justin glared at Jake defiantly. "No."

The whip cracked against his skin, and Justin let out a cry of agony.

"Are you sure?" Jake asked.

Teeth clenched, Justin snapped, "I will never join you. You're nothing but a fucking monster!"

The whip flicked along his chest again and again. His flesh split with each lick of the leather on his body. Blood soaked his jeans and dripped to the floor. Jake stopped long enough to taunt him. "You know, I was there that day. When you killed that innocent girl. Such a beautiful expression on her face when she died."

When Justin looked at him in horror, Jake smiled cruelly. "Oh, yes, I saw when you slid your sword into her body. It cut through her like butter. Pity I couldn't taste her."

Jake flayed his chest several more times. Justin whimpered when Jake stopped, hanging from the chains, unable to find the strength to stand on his own. "No," Justin whispered.

"What was that?" Jake asked.

"I didn't mean to kill her," Justin sobbed in anguish.

"But you did. And I bet, knowing you as I do, you've tormented yourself with her death all these years." Jake laughed maniacally and began whipping Justin again. "You're nothing but a weak, pathetic pup. Once the ritual is over tonight, I shall enjoy having you all to myself."

The pain became too much, and Justin passed out. When he came to later, he found there were over a hundred werewolves in the room, and they were chanting. Jake stood before them, holding some type of parchment. Justin knew it had to be the scroll Vincent had mentioned. He prayed Kara had found Vincent and the hybrid would agree to help him. They hadn't parted on the best of terms, and he didn't know if he would last once Jake really started in on him.

He found himself slipping in and out of unconsciousness as the ritual carried on. Finally, the werewolves began to leave in small groups at a time. Eventually the room emptied, and the only one left was Jake. He watched Jake place the scroll inside a box that he took from the room, and when he returned he didn't have it with him. Sheer terror inundated him as he watched Jake approach him. The thought of the fucking bastard touching him was more than he could bear. He knew he deserved worse after what he'd done, but he would rather die a thousand deaths at the hands of a hunter than be raped by the one who'd turned him.

He'd thought his fate inevitable until he heard Vincent's voice. Pure elation had spread through him when he'd realized Vincent had come to rescue him. The ensuing fight had horrified Justin, but he'd had faith in Vincent. Now they were on their way out of the city, and he could barely move his limbs from sheer exhaustion. Turning his head, he studied Vincent until Vincent glanced his way. "What's wrong?" Vincent asked.

Two simple words left his mouth. "You came."

Justin jerked in shock when Vincent grabbed his hand and entwined their fingers. "Of course I came, Justin. Did you think I'd leave you there? Besides, we have a deal, and I don't back out on my promises."

Vincent returned his attention to the road, leaving their hands tangled together. Justin stared at the way their skin appeared so different from each other. His skin shone so brightly against Vincent's darker tone. He remembered the earrings then and cried, "Wait!"

Vincent nearly swerved off the road and had to pull his hand from Justin's to control the car. "Jesus! What the hell are you trying to do? Kill us?"

"We need to go back. My things are in the hotel, and I bought a present for Kara… and you."

Vincent glanced at him, surprise shining in his eyes, before grabbing his hand again. "I took everything from the room. There was nothing else there when I left."

"Did you get the necklace and earrings from the nightstand?" he asked.

"Yes. They're in my pocket. Calm down."

Justin breathed a sigh of relief and settled back against the seat. "Where are we going?"

"I called the other hunters. They're making their way here as we speak. We are going to hole up somewhere until I hear from them." Vincent looked over at him and asked, "What happened? Why did you run off?"

"I needed time to think. So much has happened lately, and my life has changed so suddenly." Justin laughed without true mirth. "Before Kara, I had no one, and now I find myself with two people I trust and care about."

"So what happened when you got here? How'd you end up being the scratching post for that asshole?"

Wincing, Justin dropped his gaze to his hands. "The first morning there I caught the scent of more than one of them. I saw a werewolf go into the bakery and not come back out. I watched the shop for two days. There were too many to count coming and going. That's when I knew I couldn't handle it alone and called Kara to get you."

He retold of the events leading to Vincent finding him and rescuing him. Silence filled the car when he'd finished, and Justin wondered if Vincent was angry with him for having to rescue him. He didn't know if Vincent realized when he'd said there were only two people in his life, it included Vincent. Even if Vincent didn't accept anything from him, Justin trusted him and cared about him. He'd realized the truth behind his feelings for Vincent when he appeared in the doorway of the ritual room.

Vincent sighed. "I wish you would have called me before you took it upon yourself to stake the place out. You wouldn't have had to go through any of it."

Shrugging without thinking, Justin winced at the tug on his wounds and then replied, "I didn't want to call you so far from the city if there wasn't a reason for it."

Vincent gave him a look Justin couldn't read then said, "Jake is the one who bit you."

"Yes."

"Do you feel any different? I don't think I killed him. I just wanted to get us both away from there."

"No, I can still sense the wolf in me." Justin tilted his head to the side and closed his eyes. He would never admit it aloud, but the warmth of Vincent's hand in his made him feel safer than he'd felt in centuries. Did Vincent even realize their hands were still tangled together? Justin had his answer a second later when Vincent squeezed gently, his heart bolting upward to lodge in his throat. Instead of analyzing why Vincent offered him comfort, Justin just allowed himself to doze the remainder of the drive.

CHAPTER 11

W hen Vincent reached a town he thought for sure was far enough away, he pulled in front of a small motel. He didn't want to wake Justin yet and went in to book the room. The owner gave him a key to the only room they had left, one with a king-size bed. Vincent moved the car to a space in front of their room before grabbing his and Justin's things to bring inside. He went back to the car for Justin. Unbuckling him, Vincent slid an arm beneath Justin's legs and another behind his back. Though muscled and almost his same height, Justin weighed nothing in his arms.

He carried him into the room and laid him gently on the bed. He untied the laces of Justin's boots and slid them off, setting them on the floor next to the bed. Justin's hands settled on top of his when he reached to start undoing the buttons of Justin's jeans. Embarrassment colored Justin's voice as he said, "I can do it."

Vincent turned away when Justin stood from the bed to remove the blood soaked jeans. He busied himself digging into the duffle bag to grab a pair of sweats for Justin and tossed them onto the bed within Justin's reach. "Thanks," Justin murmured.

The rustling of clothing caused an uncomfortable warmth to settle in Vincent's groin. Stifling a groan, he closed his eyes and balled his hands into fists to keep from doing something stupid. He heard the bed move, alerting him to Justin sitting back down. "Can I have the necklace and earrings?" Justin asked, his voice husky.

Vincent drew the requested items from his pocket and turned around toward Justin, holding them out to him. Justin took the necklace, wrapped it in one of his shirts, and placed it in his backpack. He tensed a fraction when Justin stood and came to him, took his hand, and set the earrings into his palm, closing his fingers around them. The light blue of Justin's eyes darkened slightly with an emotion Vincent couldn't identify. "Thank you for coming to rescue me. I'm sorry I'm nothing but a pain in the ass. I saw these the other day and thought they'd suit you."

He gave Vincent a crooked smile. Vincent couldn't resist the urge in him and, without stopping to think too hard on it, he pulled Justin into his arms and kissed him. This time the kiss was soft and slow instead of hard and angry. He outlined Justin's lips with his tongue, seeking entrance. A groan rattled in Vincent's throat when Justin opened underneath him, and he tightened his hold around Justin, dipping his tongue in to taste him.

Justin wrapped his arms around Vincent's shoulders, hands coming together at the base of Vincent's neck. Vincent encouraged Justin to play by teasingly flicking his tongue against Justin's. When Justin responded, tentative and shy, Vincent deepened the kiss further, sliding his hands down to grip the cheeks of Justin's rounded bottom. A gasp issued from Justin, and Vincent squeezed the firm mounds of flesh, drawing him in tighter. He broke the kiss long enough to pull Justin to the bed and down onto it with him, never stopping to think beyond needing to feel Justin beneath him.

Vincent cupped Justin's cheek, stroking his thumb over the smooth flesh, while not relinquishing his hold on Justin's mouth. He swallowed a sigh of pleasure Justin let forth, suckling Justin's lower lip leisurely. Moving them fully onto the mattress, Vincent wedged himself between Justin's thighs and rocked his hips, grinding his hard cock along Justin's answering lust. Justin moaned in pleasure, a sound Vincent relished, and he reached down to release Justin's stiff cock. When he wrapped his fingers around the silken length, Justin wrenched free of the kiss to cry out, back arching from the bed. Vincent smeared the drop of pre-cum along the tip with his thumb before stroking the thick shaft.

The musky scent of Justin's desire tantalized Vincent's nostrils, begging him to taste Justin's essence. He pressed kisses along Justin's collarbone, sternum, and further still until he could reach Justin's straining dick. Skimming his tongue around the crown, Vincent growled the moment the flavor of pre-cum exploded against his taste buds. He sucked the tip into his mouth and swallowed the entire length of Justin's cock. Justin screamed at the abrupt move, grabbing at Vincent's head and latching on. Vincent sucked, hard, on retreat and slashed his tongue along the bottom of the shaft on his way down.

"Oh, God, Vincent," Justin mewled.

If his mouth hadn't been full, he may well have grinned arrogantly at making Justin lose control. Wanting more, Vincent stripped Justin's sweatpants from his body then nuzzled the rounded sac at the base of Justin's cock. He pulled one orb into his mouth, lapping at the rounded flesh, before releasing it to imbibe the other. A tremor worked its way through Justin's long form when Vincent trailed his tongue along the sensitive skin leading to the one place Vincent longed to be engulfed in. He traced the puckered flesh, flicking over the tight entrance again and again.

When he stiffened his tongue and pushed into Justin's body, Vincent heard a gasp from Justin followed by a mewling sound. He couldn't help but wonder if Justin had ever lain with another man or if Justin was untouched. The idea of being Justin's first caused his cock to pulse, and he added a finger to the mix, slipping it into the saliva-slickened hole. If he'd even thought this was possible, he'd have brought lube with him, but this never seemed a likely turn of events. He didn't want to hurt Justin and knew he needed to take his time stretching him.

Justin never protested or attempted to stop him even as he added a second and third digit. Vincent couldn't take anymore. He pulled free from the grasp of Justin's body, stripped away his clothing, and covered

Justin's form with his own. He brushed away the strands of Justin's hair stuck to his cheek and gazed into Justin's eyes. "If you don't want this, say so now," he said, his voice deep and husky with lust.

Instead of speaking, Justin answered by wrapping his legs around Vincent's waist and leaning up to kiss him. Vincent gave a guttural moan and nudged the head of his achingly hard cock at Justin's hole. Their kind were immune to human illnesses, a fact Vincent couldn't be more grateful for in that very moment as he slowly sank inside, without anything to dull the sensation consuming his shaft. Justin was hot, tight, and felt fucking fantastic. They were both sweating by the time Vincent buried the entire length of his cock, balls resting on Justin's ass cheeks. He gave a tentative short thrust of his hips, wrenching a gasp from Justin.

"Fuck, you feel so fucking good," Vincent growled, burying his face into the crook of Justin's neck. He began to move, slow at first, but gathering speed until their skin slapped together on each return plunge into Justin. When Justin raked his nails down his back, Vincent couldn't stop a cry of pleasure or the sharp lunge he gave.

Control no longer existed in Vincent. When Justin suddenly clenched around him and the sharp tang of cum struck Vincent's nose, he broke full body contact to be able to watch the hard jerks of Justin's cock as it spit white seed over his abdomen and belly. Vincent hammered into Justin without mercy for several more thrusts before he threw his head back with a loud shout, spilling inside Justin. Shudders rippled through Vincent with each pulse of his orgasm. His body felt boneless when he reached the end, and he dropped down atop Justin, panting and shivering.

Justin trailed a hand down the length of Vincent's spine, a tender action which caused a strange feeling in the pit of Vincent's stomach. Neither of them spoke or moved until Vincent softened enough to slip from Justin's body. They were both covered in sweat and cum, but Vincent found barely enough energy to roll them to their sides, cuddling Justin close to him. Eventually they both gave in to their exhaustion and fell into the blessed oblivion of sleep.

Vincent woke first the following morning. In their sleep, they'd shifted until Vincent was on his back, Justin plastered to his side and his head using Vincent's chest as a pillow, one arm lying across Vincent's waist. He didn't know why he'd given in to his desire to have sex with Justin, but he did know he couldn't regret it, no matter what their situation was. He tightened his arm around Justin for a second and then attempted to slide from the bed to take a shower. Justin let out a snuffled moan of frustration and burrowed further into Vincent's side. He smiled down at the crown of Justin's head and relaxed back into the mattress. He could remain there for a little while longer.

He thought back on the werewolves and hoped the majority of the hunters were already on the move. He also prayed the wolves wouldn't relocate again, but somehow he didn't think they would this time. Jake seemed egotistical enough to believe they wouldn't be able to stop him. It irritated him when he remembered the way Jake had touched Justin, the way he'd looked at Justin as if he owned him. Vincent wanted to smash the bastard's face in with a sledgehammer. The knowledge of why he had the urge to do bodily harm to Jake's perfect features should have pissed him off or at the very least made him disgusted with himself. Yet he couldn't lie to himself anymore. He cared about Justin, more than he'd cared about anyone in decades.

Justin began to awaken, and Vincent wondered if Justin would be ashamed of what they'd done.

Justin came to a fraction at a time. He didn't want to leave the warm cocoon he found himself in. A feeling he hadn't experienced since he'd been a little boy on his mother's lap invaded his soul. Peace. The chest beneath his cheek rose and fell with each breath, and Justin gave a tiny smile when he realized Vincent hadn't left. Then he frowned, wondering if Vincent regretted the night before. He raised his gaze to Vincent's face and saw his eyes were open, but he seemed lost in thought. Justin went to sit up, but Vincent tightened his hold on him and growled, "Where do you think you're going?"

"I-I was going to go take a shower," Justin stammered. Embarrassment crowded in, and his cheeks grew hot. He kept his head tucked against Vincent's chest.

Vincent used the knuckle of his index finger to raise Justin's face to his. "I hope I didn't hurt you. I know I was a little rough."

The blush already on Justin's cheeks deepened, and Justin knew his entire face had to be bright red. "I-It's okay."

"Was it your first time?" Vincent asked, running the pad of his thumb over Justin's chin.

Unable to hold Vincent's gaze for fear of being laughed at, Justin averted his eyes. "I've never been able to trust myself with anyone before."

"Look at me, little wolf," Vincent said softly. Peeking back at Vincent, Justin found nothing except warmth in the bright violet orbs. "Thank you for placing your trust in me."

Justin swallowed hard, his throat tightening with some undefined emotion, and he could only nod in response. He'd never had the chance before becoming a werewolf to indulge in sexual experiences and once he'd been turned, he never even considered it for fear of hurting or infecting someone else.

This time Vincent let him go when Justin moved to get out of the bed. Justin grabbed his duffle and scurried into the bathroom, hiding as best he could behind the bag. He knew he should have taken a shower the night before. The blood had dried on his skin and flaked off in more than one place, but he'd been too exhausted to care and then everything with Vincent had happened. He wrinkled his nose at the itchiness of dried cum and blood on his body, scratching at his lower belly. Justin looked himself over in the mirror while the water heated. The usual haunted look he'd become accustomed to no longer stared back at him. He couldn't believe the turn of events last night or how he'd slept better than he'd done since being turned.

But he knew nothing with Vincent could last. They were enemies. Right?

Sneering in disgust, Justin rushed through his shower and dressed. Vincent took one while Justin stood by the window, lost in thought over the events of the last week. He almost missed what Vincent said when Vincent returned to the room.

"We're going to remain here until I receive the call the others have arrived."

Justin nodded distractedly and almost jumped out of his skin when Vincent walked up behind him and wrapped his arms around Justin's waist. "Let's go get something to eat. There's a park I saw on the way through last night, and we'll eat there, okay?"

"Okay," Justin murmured.

They bought sushi from a nearby restaurant and drove to the park Vincent mentioned, where they found a place to sit underneath a huge tree. Justin sat with his back to the bark of the tree. The park certainly was beautiful. A small pond held a family of ducks and a couple of swans. There were two children nearby with their parents, and they were giggling in delight at the sight of the birds.

When they finished their food, Vincent leaned back on his arms, tipping his face to the sky with a sigh of contentment. "I haven't relaxed like this in a long time."

Justin turned enough to look at Vincent's profile. His beautiful white hair hung down into a pool at his rear end; Vincent hadn't braided it again after his shower. That's when Justin noticed the earring flashing in a brief shaft of sunlight through the tree branches overhead. He'd worn them. Joy blossomed in Justin's chest, delighted his gift had pleased Vincent enough to put them on. Vincent glanced at him and saw him staring. "What? Do I have soy sauce on my face?"

Ducking his head, Justin mumbled, "You're wearing them."

"Yeah."

Sneaking a look from under his lashes, Justin saw Vincent smiling. "I wasn't sure you'd want them."

"Honestly, I was surprised you even bought them for me. With the

74

way we left things before, I thought maybe I was the reason why you took off."

"No! I-I just had to sort out a lot of things in my head." Justin nervously picked at a blade of grass. "When I saw them, they immediately reminded me of you. I didn't know if you would care or even want them."

Vincent reached out, picked up Justin's hand, and raised it to his lips to place a kiss on Justin's knuckles. Justin flushed and then, much to his horror, squeaked in surprise when Vincent yanked him into his lap. Vincent chuckled at the sound but didn't do anything more than fold his arms around him and rest his chin on Justin's shoulder.

CHAPTER 12

They returned to the motel when the sun began to set, and they repeated the pattern for the next two days while they waited for Vincent's phone to ring. During the day, they chose to explore the town they were in, but the nights were spent exploring every inch of each other. Justin knew their idyllic time together couldn't last, but he absorbed every single moment with Vincent he could. He imprinted the memory of the scent of Vincent's skin, the taste of his kiss, and the feel of Vincent buried deep inside of him. They would be what he clung to when the time came for Vincent to carry through on his end of their deal.

The phone call came the third morning right after Vincent finished waking him with a leisurely bout of lovemaking. They were quiet as they packed their meager belongings and checked out of the motel. Vincent didn't take his hand this time while driving back toward the city where the nest of werewolves was. Justin couldn't stop the disappointment and hurt burrowing into his heart, but he shouldn't have expected anything beyond the two days they'd had together.

When Vincent pulled over into a rest area thirty miles outside of the city, Justin looked at him in confusion. "I thought we were heading to the bakery."

"We are, but everyone is gathering here until night fall. We'd draw too much attention if we met there."

Justin saw a group of about thirty men and women standing beneath a cluster of trees at the rest area. "Is that all of them?"

"It's only part of them. The rest are still on their way and should be here soon. Come on." Vincent exited the Challenger and walked over to the group, greeting several of them with clasped hands or hugs.

Justin hung back, nervous about being surrounded by so many hunters. He didn't know how they'd react once they knew what he was. Vincent turned to him and motioned for him to join them. "Everyone, I'm sure you've heard of the werewolf who hunts his own kind. This is Justin. He's been helping me locate the werewolves, and he's the one who found the ritual room."

All eyes turned to Justin, and he fidgeted. Then, to his shock, smiles broke out on everyone's faces, and they came to him, one by one, to greet him with handshakes or hugs. Bewilderment must have shown on his face because Vincent laughed. "They're not all like me. You'll be fine."

More and more of them began arriving until there were about sixty to seventy men and women. Justin started to get worried. There had to be at least a hundred of the wolves. "Is this enough?" he murmured to himself.

"Scared, wolf?" a nasty voice asked behind him.

Justin spun around to face Yasmine. "You didn't see how many there were," he replied defensively.

"Don't worry, mutt. We're stronger than any pack of dogs like you." She leaned in close to Justin and said, "I don't trust you, and I hope you don't think laying a trap will work."

"No matter what you think, I'm trying to help Vincent and the rest of you. Don't worry, once this is over I'll be dead anyway," he replied and walked away.

He sank down onto a bench and sighed, staring at the ground. Vincent sat beside him a few minutes later. "You ready? We're going in tonight."

Justin dug his nails into the wooden plank beneath him. "Maybe I shouldn't go."

"What? Why?" Vincent demanded.

"Because they fear me. Even the ones who greeted me when we first got here do. I could smell it on them." Justin frowned. "Besides, it's not like I've been very successful lately at being able to handle myself. I'll be nothing but a burden. Someone could get hurt because of me."

Vincent growled in anger. "It doesn't matter what they believe. You want the same as we do. To stop those monsters and get the scroll back. You handle yourself better than you give yourself credit for. When it's three against one, it's unfair odds. You promised to help, and I am going to hold you to that promise!" Vincent stood and started walking back to the others.

"You think it's so easy, don't you?" Justin yelled at him. "You think it's nothing more than three against one? Or that it's nothing more than a deal I made with you? Vincent, you hate me, too. Remember your promise? You may sleep with me because you're horny or whatever other excuse you conjure in your head, but it still comes down to the fact that at the end of the day, you'll kill me. So I'll go keep my end of the deal so you'll keep yours!"

Justin had never been so angry or scared before. He feared for himself, but also for Vincent. The hunters were outnumbered, and they could all be killed. He could be forced to watch Vincent die before Jake tortured him to death. Every emotion exploded through him, building inside of him, and Justin felt the itching beneath his skin, the same one he felt every full moon. The beast wanted out! "Vin—" Justin broke off in pain, his bones beginning to break and reform.

He watched Vincent shrink only to realize Vincent wasn't shrinking, he was growing. Justin waited for himself to black out like he always did once the transformation began. Yet he didn't. Vincent turned back only to watch with horror etched on his face while Justin went through the change. The hair along his body ruffled in the breeze, and he lifted his hands only to see huge clawed paws in their place. Panic enveloped him and then he saw the look in Vincent's eyes. Justin couldn't stand to see the disgust forming. The others were running toward them, but Vincent held out his arm to stop the hunters. "Justin?" he asked hesitantly.

Justin felt a tear slip out of his eye and drop off the end of the long, monstrous snout where his mouth once was. He spun and tore into the bushes. Branches and leaves scraped over him as he ran. He didn't know how'd been able to change or how to return to human. Now he had control of himself in the monstrous form! Maybe the spell had affected him even though he'd been unconscious.

He ran until the agony of knowing what a monster he was brought him to his knees. Throwing his head back, he howled in grief and anguish. His claws dug into the soil beneath him, and he raged, roaring once more. So caught up in his torment, he didn't hear Vincent approach. A hand came down gently on his shoulder, and Vincent dropped down beside him. "It's okay, Justin."

Even with conscious thought, he still couldn't speak in this form, and he could only shake his head.

"I kind of anticipated something like this," Vincent told him. "You may have been blacked out, but the spell would still have an effect on you."

The anger had long since been replaced by despair, and Justin felt his body starting the shift. He grunted when his bones reshaped themselves once more. After, he lay there, his head in Vincent's lap, staring at the trees and sky above. Vincent proved to be more astute than Justin gave him credit for. "You're scared of him."

Justin closed his eyes, cheeks hot with embarrassment. "Yes."

"It's okay to be scared. It's what makes you human." Justin opened his eyes in surprise. Vincent smiled at him, one so tender Justin had to blink to make sure he didn't imagine it. "Yeah, I said human. When tonight is over, you will no longer have to fear him. We're going to kill him, Justin, and then you'll be human again."

Vincent carded his fingers through Justin's hair. "And then I won't have to hold up my end of the deal." He paused for a second and then continued, "For what it's worth, I don't hate you. What we did these last few days… it's not just about being horny or whatever excuse I can come up with." Vincent tossed his words back at Justin.

"I—" Justin would have responded, but Vincent bent to capture Justin's lips with his own.

Sighing with pleasure, Justin lost himself in the kiss, his body hardening with lust. Vincent's reaction to their kiss dug in between Justin's shoulder blades. Vincent twisted them until he lay on top of Justin, their hard chests pressing together. He reached between them to fondle Justin through the frayed remnants of his jeans.

"We should… ah… get back," Justin gasped.

"Why?" Vincent slid his mouth down to Justin's neck and lightly licked at the sensitive skin there.

Lust washed over Justin as he struggled to reply. "The-They'll be looking for us."

"No. They won't." With that, Vincent captured one of Justin's nipples in his mouth, and Justin lost all sense of reason to the desire clouding his mind.

He held Vincent's head closer to him and couldn't stifle a cry when Vincent nibbled gently on his nipple. Justin needed to feel Vincent's skin. He grabbed at Vincent's shirt, yanking on it. Vincent took the hint, pulled away long enough to strip the shirt off, and then dropped down again to feast upon Justin's chest. Justin ran his hands down the strong, rippling muscles in Vincent's back.

They scrambled to remove the remainder of their clothing until they lay naked on their sides, Justin's back pressed to Vincent's front. Vincent nuzzled the back of Justin's neck, and Justin couldn't stifle a giggle. "What's wrong?" Vincent whispered into his ear.

"You're tickling me."

Vincent rocked his hips, digging his stiff cock into the crease of Justin's backside. "Is that tickling you?"

Justin moaned and arched against him. He reached behind him to grab onto Vincent's rock hard thigh and turned his head to lick tenderly at Vincent's mouth. Vincent caught his tongue with his lips and sucked it hungrily into his mouth while one firm hand caressed along Justin's side until he reached the one place they both wanted Vincent to be. A tremble shook Justin's body when Vincent breached his hole with two saliva-slick fingers. "Even after the last two days, you're still tight as hell," Vincent growled and nipped the shell of Justin's ear.

When Vincent thrust those two fingers deep into him, Justin groaned in pleasure. But Vincent, who was as desperate as Justin for more, quickly spat into his hand and slathered his length before replacing his fingers with the blunt head of his cock. "Let me in, baby," Vincent murmured, pushing forward and sinking into Justin.

They let out a collective moan when Vincent bottomed out. Justin dug his nails into the thigh beneath his hand as Vincent began thrusting, surging in and pulling almost entirely free of Justin. Vincent added to the sensations bombarding Justin's senses by wrapping his hand around Justin's prick and milking him in rhythm of his strokes. "Oh, God," Justin moaned, unable to stop from pushing back and silently begging for more.

Vincent moved faster and harder, moaning Justin's name along with several other epithets. Justin dug his nails further into Vincent's thigh the closer he got to the edge of his orgasm. Both of their moans and cries got louder, no doubt echoing through the trees around them. It only took a few more of Vincent's hard lunges to send him flying. "Vincent!" he screamed as he fell over into the abyss.

He barely registered the growl of his own name when Vincent followed him, but he did pull Vincent tighter to him, ensuring every drop of spend remained inside of him. Finally, they both stilled. Vincent kissed the nape of his neck in a gentle brush of his lips and pulled free of Justin's body. He carefully turned Justin to face him and cupped his cheek, stroking his thumb over the high cheekbone.

Justin moved the scant inches between them to kiss Vincent, closing his eyes to hide the tears threatening to fall. In two hundred years, he'd never had a reason to want to continue living, but he knew he couldn't be selfish. Vincent deserved more, deserved better. He needed someone who didn't turn into an uncontrollable monster three nights a month, someone he could be proud to be with him, someone stronger than Justin could ever hope to be. But he wanted these memories to take away and greedily clung to Vincent, burying his face against Vincent's chest.

When Vincent stirred, Justin reluctantly released his hold on him and sat up. He ran a hand through his hair to straighten it a bit and then looked around for what remained of his clothes after he'd shifted. Vincent handed him the shredded jeans, the only remaining article of his. "Should probably think about buying stock in a clothing company because it's always being ripped off of you," Vincent joked.

"After tonight, it won't matter because I'll either be human or dead." Justin didn't look at him as he returned the way they'd come from.

CHAPTER 13

Vincent stared after Justin and sighed. The other hunters hadn't understood why he didn't want to just kill Justin, but everything had changed. He knew, despite the beast beneath the surface, Justin had a kind heart and wanted nothing more than to help. His feelings for Justin had changed as well. He couldn't imagine taking his sword to Justin now. He regretted the agreement, and he hoped by the time the battle tonight was over Jake would be dead and Justin would be human.

Trailing after Justin, he sifted through the last couple of weeks since Justin had entered his life; the day they'd met, the way Justin's scent called to him, Justin's fierce protectiveness of Kara, their stolen moments in the dark, and the earrings Justin had gifted him. He touched the one in his right earlobe. His emotions went haywire the second his finger grazed the purple stone. Vincent froze where he was when a thought he'd never expected in his life struck him right in the chest.

Could he possibly... love Justin? His mind rebelled at the idea of caring for one of the monsters he'd made it his life's mission to destroy, but his heart beat fierce and wild with the knowledge of his true feelings. Justin had Vincent's heart in his hands irrevocably. There could be no way for him to carry out his end of the bargain they'd made, no matter the outcome of the upcoming fight.

Vincent resumed walking, still lost in his internal war over his emotions. When he exited the tree line, it took a few breaths to register the scene in front of him. Yasmine was on Justin's back, raining blows wherever she could reach. Rage poured through Vincent, and he rushed forward, grabbed Yasmine, and threw her to the ground. He stood over her, chest heaving in his fury. "What the fuck is wrong with you, Yasmine?"

"I can smell you on him and him on you. You're disgusting. Rutting with a werewolf? How could you?" Yasmine screamed, tears filling her eyes.

Pity for her set in, and Vincent crouched beside her. "My feelings for you have never been anything more than friends, Yas. Even if I was *rutting*, as you so elegantly put it, you have no right to me or a say in what I do. Justin has done nothing wrong, and you need to understand your actions are pushing me away." Vincent straightened and stared down at her, shaking his head. "I think you need to grow up a little more and realize it's a harsh world. You can't always get what you want."

With those words, he turned, grabbed Justin by the arm, and led him away, leaving Yasmine sitting on the ground.

The hunters continued to gather at the rest stop. The sheer volume of them made Justin's head spin. He'd never known there were so many. He wasn't sure how he'd gone as many years as he had without running into more of them.

One of the hunters went ahead to scout the area to see if the werewolves were still there. When the report came back that they were, Justin knew tonight would decide the rest of his life.

"I'm surprised they didn't try to leave," Vincent murmured.

"I'm not. Jake's arrogance wouldn't allow them to run. He believes he can't be hurt."

Vincent growled low. "That arrogance will be his downfall tonight."

Justin hoped so because the selfish part of him wanted to stay at Vincent's side. The plan would be to wait for nightfall, for the city to sleep, then slip in under the cover of darkness. Justin knew Jake would be ready for them, no matter when they went, but the late hour would prevent human casualties caught in the crossfire.

Groups were formed while they waited, and food was passed among them to fortify everyone's strength. Justin rested beside Vincent, leaning against a tree. They didn't talk, just sat in silence, their hands tangled together out of sight of the others. Nervous energy built faster the quicker the hours passed. The sun hung low in the horizon when everyone began to move. They left at separate times, wanting to prevent drawing as much attention to themselves as they could. When it was their turn to go, Vincent gave a small squeeze of Justin's hand in reassurance and then released him to stand up.

The ride to the little town was also made without talking. By the time darkness had fallen completely, the groups of hunters had reached their destination. The street the bakery resided on appeared deserted. No lights shone from any window, and the entire area seemed shrouded in darkness. An eerie feeling trickled down Justin's spine, and he frowned, surprised not a single building appeared to have anyone still in it. It wasn't exactly a Tokyo-sized city, but the businesses definitely didn't close their doors before nine. "Something's not right," Justin murmured when they passed the little store he'd purchased the earrings and necklace in. "Where is everyone?"

"The scroll Jake has isn't the only one, Justin," Vincent replied. "The hunters have come into possession of a number of magical artifacts as well, including spells that urge humans to stay away from an area and to turn their attention from our actions. We use them when we have to clean up after preternatural attacks. The moment we entered the city, one of these spells was triggered. I guess you could say everyone found it impossible to remain in a two block radius of the bakery."

Justin raised his brows at Vincent. He'd had no idea about such things, though he had known there were other malevolent creatures besides werewolves. He'd killed a few warlocks and vampires over the years, mostly because they had gotten in his way while hunting.

Most of the hunters abandoned their vehicles a few blocks over, choosing to approach on foot. Vincent left the Charger at the end of the street where the bakery resided, and they joined with a small group of hunters already waiting nearby.

The werewolves were ready for them as Justin expected. There were a number of the beasts hiding in the shadows, and the hunters spread out around the area. Justin gripped his sword tighter, knowing he couldn't hesitate tonight or else someone could get hurt or worse, killed. A shout behind the two of them brought Vincent and Justin around to find several of the hunters already engaged in battle. Werewolves leapt from the top of buildings, from the open alley ways, and out of the various buildings around them. Justin cried out a warning to a hunter when they didn't seem to notice one of the creatures approaching from behind. The hunter sidestepped the attack and spun around to spear it straight through the heart.

The unknown hunter gave him a quick nod of thanks and returned to fighting another werewolf. Seeing the deft, accurate way the hunters were moving and battling the monsters caused Justin to feel a little better about their chances to end this tonight. He resumed following Vincent, eyes trained on the long braid swinging against Vincent's back while he walked. His heart clenched with fear for Vincent. The idea of him being hurt or dying scared Justin out of his mind. He didn't want to lose the only other person who meant the world to him besides Kara.

They were halfway to the bakery when they were charged by two werewolves. Standing back to back, they faced off against the beasts. Justin realized mid-fight the only way to finish this was to kill Jake. If Jake was killed, the rest would disband. They needed a leader, an alpha, to follow. Without Jake, the pack would fall apart. "Vincent," Justin yelled, his sword caught between the claws of the beast he fought.

"What?" Vincent shouted, dodging a claw flying toward his face.

"Jake has to be in the ritual room. If we kill him, the rest will run.

I'm going." Justin plunged his sword straight into the werewolf's heart, piercing it with the silver blade. He tugged it free and, as the body fell, rushed toward the bakery alley entrance.

"Justin, wait!" He heard Vincent scream behind him but ignored him and kept moving, dodging around multiple werewolves until he burst through the back door. He raced into the kitchen toward the freezer and wrenched it open. Practically flying down the steps, Justin almost lost his footing more than once. His eyes took several precious seconds to adjust to the darkness, and he almost didn't see the creature running toward him.

Justin swung out, his sword connecting with the monster's neck, cleanly slicing it free from its body. The werewolf hadn't even hit the floor when Justin took off running again. When he came to an abrupt halt at the ritual room, his boots fought for purchase on the slick concrete, and he had to grab the doorframe to keep from falling. Jake stood at the pedestal, still in human form, when Justin darted into the room. "Ah, I see my pet has returned to me," Jake said, smirking.

"It's over, Jake. You're going to die tonight, even if I have to die with you!" Justin shouted, rushing toward Jake, sword ready.

Jake sidestepped and swung a fist at Justin, catching him in the face. Justin couldn't stop himself as he flew through the air, hitting the wall with a loud crash. There was no way Jake should be so strong in human form. The spell must unlock more than their ability to shift.

"Haven't you learned yet, Justin?" Jake stalked to where Justin lay gasping for air. "Your strength is no match for mine."

"Maybe not, but mine is," Vincent snarled, stepping into the chamber.

Jake narrowed his eyes and turned to glare at Vincent. "You again! No matter. Once I've killed you, Justin won't have his protector anymore, and then I'll show him what true pain is."

Justin struggled to stand, his back aching from the impact with the wall. When Jake started to shift, Justin stared in horror. The seams on his clothes popped the larger he grew, limbs lengthening and hair sprouting all over his body. Fully transformed, he stood seven and a half feet tall. Jake roared at Vincent, saliva dripping from his huge fangs. Vincent pointed his sword at Jake and said, "I will kill you for what you've done to Justin. You're a foul creature and need to return to the hell you came from."

Vincent struck at Jake, but Jake caught the sword in one huge claw. Justin couldn't look away when Jake wrenched the sword from Vincent and flung it away from them. It landed with a clatter across the room, close to the pedestal. Without warning, Jake slammed into Vincent, sending him airborne toward the wall behind him. Justin screamed in terror when Vincent's head snapped forward from the impact, knocking him unconscious.

Fury swarmed Justin as he watched Vincent crash to the ground and lay unmoving. The centuries of bitterness and resentment toward Jake sparked his rage even further. Before he knew it, he started to shift, faster than he ever had in the past. In seconds, he stood fully transformed, his body trembling with emotion. He snarled at Jake, who'd turned around when he'd heard Justin moving behind him. The muscles in Justin's thick, muscular legs bunched as he propelled himself across the chamber to attack Jake.

Claws slashing at each other, they danced a tango of hatred and wrath. Blood welled up from every cut, every slice, spattering across the floor. Justin took out two centuries of self-loathing, fear, and anger at his life being stolen from him in those moments. He wanted Jake to know the depth of those emotions eating at his soul since that fateful night. The hunters appearing in the doorway barely registered with him, his focus entirely on Jake and ensuring the bastard paid for everything he'd done.

Jake rammed a clawed fist at Justin's chest, trying to punch through to crush his heart. It caught Justin off guard and, though unsuccessful, the impact knocked him to the ground. Jake whirled and stomped toward Vincent. Justin realized Vincent had come to and now held the scroll in his hands. He struggled to his feet, but not in time to get to them. Vincent bolted out of the ritual room and down the tunnel, Jake hot on his heels.

Justin tried to follow, but a scream from Yasmine stopped him in his tracks. One of the creatures had her by the throat, holding her in the air with one claw poised to make a death strike. A split second was all it took for him to drop the chase and hurry over to help her.

CHAPTER 14

Vincent's footsteps echoed through the tunnel, the sound loud and booming with his mad dash out of the ritual room. He flew up the stairs and through the bakery to the street behind the shop. Jake wasn't far behind him. Vincent spun to face off with Jake, sword at the ready. The doorway was too small, and Jake smashed through the frame, sending debris raining to the ground. Once free of the building, Jake drew himself to his full height, fire snapping from his eyes at Vincent as they circled one another. "Why don't you change back to your human form, Jake? Or are you too scared to face me in your weaker form?"

Jake growled at him and began to change right there on the street. Once in his human half, he taunted, "You think you can beat me, hybrid?"

"I know I can," Vincent replied cockily. He'd realized what Justin hadn't. Jake lusted for Justin, the one thing he couldn't have, with every fiber of his being. It drove Jake crazy that Justin wouldn't submit to him. "I mean, after all, I beat you already."

Feigned amusement caused Jake to smirk at him. "Oh? How is that?"

Pausing, Vincent studied Jake, letting him dangle for a long moment. Then he said, "I won Justin."

Those three words served their purpose, sending Jake into a furious rage again and forcing his hand. It gave Vincent the opening he'd been waiting for. He didn't move as Jake rushed him, but at the last possible second, he brought his sword in line with Jake's heart. Jake couldn't stop himself in time and impaled himself on the sword. The silver went straight through and out of Jake's back.

Surprise and pain flooded Jake's eyes as he staggered a few steps away from Vincent. "Well," blood started seeping from the corner of Jake's mouth, "ain't that a bitch."

Jake crumpled to the ground, body still. Vincent stood over him for a moment, then extracted his sword and turned to go back into the bakery. Entering the ritual room, his gaze immediately settled on Justin, who'd already returned to human form, and Vincent breathed a sigh of relief Justin hadn't been hurt. It surprised him though when Yasmine accepted the hand Justin held out to her. She had multiple deep scratches on her arms and legs and another across her cheek. Justin stripped off the fragments of his shirt and helped stem the flow of blood.

"Justin," Vincent said, stepping to his side.

Justin looked at him, and something in his face must have told Justin what they both wanted. Tears filled Justin's eyes, and he whispered, "It's finally over."

Vincent nodded and placed his hand on Justin's shoulder, squeezing gently. The two of them flanked Yasmine, helping her out of the ritual room. There were bodies everywhere, werewolves and hunters alike. Vincent could feel the sadness radiating from Justin when they passed a dark-haired hunter holding another and crying.

"So much death," Justin murmured.

Another hunter lay broken almost in half by the entrance to the tunnel. Vincent knew it would take a long time for the hunters to recover from this. "They will be honored, Justin."

Justin gave him a haunted look filled with grief and guilt. Then it faded to resolve, and he helped Yasmine lean on Vincent. "I need to see him. I need to know for sure."

Vincent watched Justin exit the bakery, knowing he needed peace of mind, and gladly supported Yasmine to give him that. Only, he heard Justin give a cry of anguish seconds later, and Vincent swung Yasmine into his arms and hurried from the building. His eyes widened when he saw Justin on his knees with his face in his hands. Jake's body was gone. Nothing remained except a large blood stain.

He set Yasmine down carefully to lean on the building and walked slowly over to Justin's side. Vincent placed his hand on Justin's shoulder, but Justin stood abruptly, knocking his hand away. "We need to help the others," Justin said stiffly and headed around to the front of the bakery.

Staring after him, Vincent felt unease settle into his belly. He turned to help Yasmine, and they made their way to the main street as well. Neither one of them could stifle their reaction to the sight which lay before them. There were significant losses on their side. At least twenty hunters lay scattered along the sidewalks and street. Crying and moans of pain could be heard in every direction. It reminded Vincent of walking onto a battlefield when the war ended.

The first steps would need to be to clear the streets, burn the bodies of the werewolves, and accomplish this before the humans awoke. Sunrise wasn't far off, a matter of hours, and the spell would dissipate at dawn. Vincent helped tend to the wounded and would occasionally glimpse Justin, covered in blood and sweat, hauling away another werewolf. He could already smell the acrid scent of burning flesh from the fire they'd built in several dumpsters behind the buildings. The bodies of the hunters were carried to the cars waiting nearby and gently settled in the back seats or truck beds. They would be given a hunter's funeral.

When Vincent finished tending the last of the wounded, he joined Justin where he stood watching the blaze. "Justin—"

Justin interrupted him. "I need to say goodbye to Kara."

"Goodbye?" Vincent asked.

"He isn't dead." Justin's voice held no emotion, flat and stone cold.

Vincent knew what Justin meant, but he didn't want to think about it. He knew he would never be able to go through with killing Justin. The thought of Justin being one of those lifeless bodies in the streets out front made him shudder, and pain shafted through his heart. He had to find a way to convince Justin to go on living.

The pink fingers of dawn crept along the sky as the remainder of the destruction of their battle was cleared away. Most of the hunters had already left, and Vincent and Justin were the last to leave, taking the time to break up the charred remains in the dumpsters to prevent the humans from finding the bodies. Covered in soot, blood, and God knew what else, they returned to Vincent's Challenger and headed back toward Tokyo by mid-afternoon. It would take at least a couple of hours to reach home, but they didn't speak the entire trip, both lost in their thoughts.

Throughout their journey, Vincent would glance at Justin every so often. He could see the resolution in Justin's face and the air of sadness clinging to the younger man. A sense of panic set in. How could he persuade Justin not to leave him? He couldn't lie to himself or deny his feelings anymore. He loved Justin, and he wouldn't let him go, not without a fight. Like Justin, he'd been alone for so long he'd forgotten how to let someone in. Even his friendships hadn't touched his heart the same way Justin had. *Maybe this was how my father felt all those years ago*, he thought to himself.

∾

They reached the city limits an hour or so before sunset, Vincent driving noticeably slower the closer they got to Tokyo, but Justin didn't waste any time the minute they entered the city. "Take me back to the house. I need to talk to Kara."

Thankfully Kara was home when they got to the house. He knew saying goodbye would be hard, but he owed her at least that much. "You can come in if you want," he said to Vincent.

Kara gave a cry of happiness when he walked in the front door. Tears started rolling down her cheeks, and she ran to him, flinging her arms around him and hugging him tightly. Justin slipped his own around her and returned the hug. He held her for several long moments, breathing in the strawberry shampoo she loved. When he leaned away to smile sadly at her, Kara's eyes widened. "No," she whispered.

Justin could only nod. She didn't release him when he tried to release her. "You can't, Justin. Please. Don't do this."

He cupped her cheek and leaned his forehead against hers. "I have no choice. The thought of me ever hurting you tears me to pieces inside. I love you, Kara. So much. If I ever got out of the cage, or we didn't get the door closed fast enough, it would be the worst thing I've ever done in my life.

"It broke my heart to leave my little sister all those years ago, but when I met you, it felt as though she had come back to me. You're the only reason I have lived until now. The morning you found me was the morning I intended to kill myself."

Kara gasped and a sob broke free. He'd never told her that before. Justin took the silver necklace he'd bought for her from his pocket and placed it around her neck. A crescent moon with one small rhinestone at the top, shaped like a star, dangled at the end. "You are the starlight in my darkness," he whispered into her hair.

"I love you, Justin. I know you don't love me the same way, but I can't live without you in my life. Please don't leave me alone. We can still find him. We'll search until the ends of the earth."

Justin shook his head. "I'm sorry, Kara."

He pressed a kiss to the crown of her hair and went to step away. She stopped him. "Grant me one thing before you leave."

"Anything," Justin pledged without hesitation.

"Kiss me." She lifted her face toward his.

Justin settled his lips over hers. The salt of her tears gave it a bitter-sweet taste. He gently pulled free. With one last look at her, he turned and said, "Let's go."

Kara's cries of sorrow chased them from the house, and Justin's throat tightened, tears stinging his eyes. He hated himself for hurting her now, but knew she deserved more than a monster who couldn't even give her his heart. Not when his heart already belonged to another.

Vincent drove them to his apartment building, and Justin went straight to the roof. He stood at the edge, looking out over the city, waiting for the last rays of the sun to disappear behind the horizon. Vincent came to stand beside him, no words spoken. When night finally fell, Justin turned to him. "Do it."

Vincent let his sword fall to the ground, the clatter causing Justin to flinch. "No."

"You swore!"

Vincent shook his head. "I won't do it. You've been able to survive for ten years by locking yourself into the cage. You can continue to do it until we can finally put Jake down."

"No!" Justin cried and moved toward Vincent, stopping when Vincent retreated. "You promised, Vincent. You have to! I can't do this anymore."

Justin sank to his knees and bowed his head. "You promised."

"It was different then. I can't do it."

Justin looked up at him. "How? How is it different?"

"I was blinded by my own hate so much that I couldn't see what was right in front of my eyes."

"What?"

"Did it ever occur to you to ask how I could possibly be a hybrid?" Vincent asked instead of answering his question.

Justin shook his head, and Vincent sat beside him. He took one of Justin's fists into his hand and splayed Justin's fingers out, one by one, then laced his with Justin's. "I'm going to tell you now because I want you to live, and I will tell you why I want you to live when I've finished with how a hybrid is possible."

"All right," Justin whispered.

CHAPTER 15

"I was born three hundred and fifteen years ago." Vincent heard Justin's sharp intake of breath. "Yes, I'm almost a hundred years older than you. My mother worked in a whore house, and this one man started coming to see her almost every night."

Vincent traced the backs of Justin's fingers, learning the dips and divots and various scars littering his hand. "I haven't told anyone this ever. I'm a little afraid you might be disgusted by what happened."

Justin surprised him by leaning over to softly nuzzle at his throat. Vincent swallowed at the contact and breathed in Justin's scent. He continued in a low voice. "My mother told me everything as she lay dying. The man, according to her, loved her very much. He talked about taking her away from that life. At first, she didn't believe him because she'd heard it all from others in the heat of the moment.

"When he kept returning, she began to believe it. She was a beautiful woman who'd wound up in a bad way when her first husband passed away. She'd had nowhere else to go. Her hair, raven's wing black, hung to her waist when she didn't have it styled in a fancy way." Vincent smiled in memory of his mother. "Her eyes were violet like mine, and she was never without a smile, even despite the distaste the townspeople had for her. They would throw stones or say awful things to her when she would walk through the town."

Vincent twisted his lips in remembered pain. "I was five the first time she came back from buying cloth and had a huge gash across her forehead. Blood had run into her eyes and dripped onto the new fabric she'd bought. I remember being terrified she would die from how much blood covered her face."

Justin made a noise of sympathy in his throat and pressed in close to Vincent's side. Vincent squeezed his hand and continued. "She became pregnant only a few months after she met my father. She told him about me, and he claimed to be ecstatic. He demanded she leave with him, but she refused because she still didn't trust him completely. Six months into the pregnancy, he told her the truth of what he was. At first, she thought him mad, but eventually she began to believe him. Horrified, she demanded he leave and never return.

"At first, he tried to argue with her, telling her he loved her and their child, and he never wanted to live without her. She couldn't control her fear of him, and she started screaming, throwing things at him." Vincent's throat grew tight, and he struggled to carry on. "She told me when she saw his eyes just before he left, she knew she'd broken his heart. She tried to go after him, to beg him for forgiveness, but she fainted from the stress, and by the time she regained consciousness he was gone. He never returned, but she said she felt his presence sometimes, as though he watched over us."

He released a sigh of sadness. "As I grew up, the other children would taunt me, and the adults were cruel in their words to me. Being the son of a whore did not bother me. But the older I got I started to gain certain... abilities. People feared me. They thought the devil had possessed me, and they would drag their children away from me if I walked by.

"When I turned ten, the butcher caught me stealing food because we were too poor to buy any. He strung me up between two poles in his yard and brought out a whip. He cut the shirt from my body as a crowd of bystanders began to gather. The butcher started whipping me, over and over. Eventually skin began to tear away with each lash. My entire back side was covered in blood, and I couldn't even move by the time my mother rushed in to stop him."

Tears were running down Justin's cheeks, and Vincent wiped them away with the back of his index finger. "That's so awful," Justin whispered.

"She died when I was twelve. She caught consumption from one of her customers. I blamed my father for everything. For leaving, my mother dying, everything. Her last words before she died were 'Don't let your anger control you. It will only lead to more suffering.' I didn't listen to her. My hatred toward him festered inside of me.

"No one in the town wanted to take me in because they were frightened of me, so they sold me into a slave trade." He stopped when Justin gave a sound of distress. "I told you it wasn't pretty."

"None of it was your fault! You were a child! How could they do that?" Justin demanded.

Vincent's heart swelled at the anger Justin exhibited on his behalf. "It's okay, little wolf. It was actually a blessing for me. If I'd stayed there, they would have eventually ended up killing me out of fear. I wound up being sold to a very hard and cruel man. He bought me to do chores on his farm. If I didn't do what he asked, he'd whip me much like the butcher had. Even though I couldn't scar because of my healing ability, every single beating left those scars on my soul. Eventually the anger became so great I ran away from the farmer, and I went to find my father.

"I started to go crazy with the hatred in me for my father. It drove me, and I became a jaded and bitter person. I would kill anyone who pissed me off." Justin leaned back to stare at him in shock. He didn't respond to the look, just kept talking. "I didn't know about the immortality then, but as the years passed and I stopped aging beyond the appearance of a twenty-five-year-old, I knew something was wrong. For a hundred years I searched for the son of a bitch. Eventually, I ran into someone who had known him. It turned out, not long after my mother died, he killed himself. When he discovered my mother had died he drove a silver knife straight through his own heart.

"By then, I'd already killed so many people that word got to the hunters about me. They had never heard of a werewolf and a human having a child together. I was arrested for murder, several of them, and they made a deal with me. If I would fight for them, for their purpose, they would give me a full pardon; otherwise, they would sentence me to death. At first, I fought against it, but eventually I gave in and joined them. I've been with them ever since. Every time I take down one of those monsters, it's like an atonement for the blood on my soul."

Vincent waited, tense, for Justin to condemn him, but when he didn't say anything, he glanced at the younger werewolf. Justin appeared lost in thought and then suddenly looked at him. "How would any of what happened to you change the way I view you? You're amazing, and you truly care that you hurt those people. Anger and despair make us do things sometimes we later regret. You've spent almost your entire life hunting werewolves and in doing so possibly saved hundreds of lives. Even if those people aren't aware of it, you're a hero."

He smiled at Justin. "Do you hear your own words?"

"What?"

"Did you even hear what you just said?"

Justin didn't respond at first and then his eyes widened when Vincent's implication sank in. "It's... different for you."

"How? I had more control over myself than you did. I *knew* what I was doing. You didn't. It's different because I had a choice, and you had none. Justin, you've done the exact same as I have and hunted werewolves for years. You've saved more lives than you have taken. Only you can choose to fight the darkness in you, Justin."

"Why do you want me to live so badly?" Justin asked.

Vincent took a deep breath. He was about to tell him something he'd never told another person in his entire life and, for the first time since he'd become a hunter, he found himself scared shitless. He opened his mouth to tell Justin, but a group of teenagers looking to party burst out onto the rooftop. Growling in frustration, he grabbed Justin's hand. "Come with me."

He led Justin downstairs to his apartment and shut the door behind them. Justin walked to stand by the window and waited for Vincent to continue. When Vincent hesitated, Justin asked, "What's wrong?"

Stalling for time, Vincent stalked toward Justin and crowded him against the wall by the window. He pressed Justin's hands to either side of his head and leaned in to kiss him. His mouth worked gently over Justin's, and he flicked his tongue out to trace the outline of Justin's lips. Justin sighed in pleasure, opening under Vincent without any hesitation. Vincent leaned away enough to see Justin's face. The usual light blue of Justin's eyes had darkened to a stormy blue.

He let go of one of Justin's hands to trace the line of Justin's jaw with one finger. "I wanted to tell you why I want you to keep fighting, and it may be a selfish reason, but it's mine, and I wouldn't change it." Still afraid of how vulnerable those three words would make him, Vincent buried his face against the side of Justin's neck. "I love you," he whispered.

CHAPTER 16

S tunned, Justin's emotions went wild, racing between disbelief to amazed to 'holy shit what the hell did he just say'. He struggled to process what Vincent had whispered. Tears started to form, and one slid down his cheek, dripping onto Vincent's neck. Vincent jerked away and saw him crying. "Aw, hell. I'm sorry, Justin. I shouldn't have sprung it on you like that."

Justin couldn't speak and merely shook his head while the tears flowed faster. Vincent pulled him closer to his chest. "What's wrong, Justin? Talk to me."

He stood and guided Justin to the bed, where he sat and pulled Justin into his lap. Gently rocking, he held him close until Justin's tears had slowed. "I—" Justin stopped to catch his breath. "I can't believe you l-love me," he said.

Vincent smiled and nuzzled Justin's temple. "I do. I've never felt about anyone the way I do about you. The thought of killing you..." he trailed off.

Justin dropped his forehead to Vincent's shoulder. Vincent's declaration caused so many new feelings to thrive within him. The primary emotion caused him to tremble, a reaction Vincent didn't miss. "Justin?"

Swallowing hard, Justin said, "It scares me. To have someone love me—"

Vincent interrupted him. "But Kara loves you."

"You didn't let me finish," Justin mumbled.

"Oh."

Justin took a minute to gather his courage. He closed his eyes and drew in a deep breath, which he blew out on a sigh. Telling someone they had your heart in their hands wasn't easy. Justin finally managed to force the words he needed to say out. "To have someone love me as much as I love them. I'm afraid it'll disappear. That you'll disappear."

"It'll never disappear because I have no intention of going anywhere," Vincent told him, his voice husky with emotion.

He used thumb and forefinger to tilt Justin's head up until their eyes met. "I do love you, you know," Vincent said.

Heat flooded Justin's cheeks, and he knew his face had to be bright red. Vincent laughed gently. "You're really adorable when you're embarrassed. It makes me want to see if that blush goes any lower."

Justin saw Vincent's eyes darken, obvious desire in their depths, and he brushed several strands of Vincent's hair away from his face. Vincent grabbed his hand and pressed a kiss to the middle of his palm. He kissed his way along Justin's fingers to the tips and, looking Justin straight in the eyes, slid Justin's index finger into his mouth. A gasp burst from Justin as heat settled into his loins, and his cock grew hard in his jeans. "Vincent," Justin whispered.

Vincent shifted Justin until he sat astride his lap and held onto Justin's hips, fingers splayed out. "Kiss me," Vincent said.

Linking his hands at the base of Vincent's neck, Justin leaned in to do exactly what Vincent wanted. He skimmed his lips over Vincent's, but Vincent didn't let him get away with the light caress. Tightening his hold on Justin's hips, he captured Justin's mouth with his, tongue flicking along the seam seeking entrance. A low moan rumbled in Vincent's chest when Justin granted him access, lips parting and tongue sliding out to meet Vincent's.

When Vincent pushed down on Justin's hips while grinding the obvious bulge in his jeans against Justin's ass, Justin growled and deepened the kiss. He whimpered in protest when Vincent broke away only to groan when Vincent latched onto a patch of skin at his throat. Vincent nipped at it, then bathed the bruised flesh with his tongue to take away the sting. Their hands began to explore, Vincent's slipping beneath Justin's shirt to map the strong lines of Justin's back while Justin's splayed over Vincent's broad shoulders.

Justin massaged the hard muscles under his palms. The need to feel skin instead of cloth brought Justin to grab hold of the shirt and tug it over Vincent's head. No matter how many times he'd seen their skin against one another, Justin still marveled over the difference of his pale complexion and Vincent's tanned warmth. "I want to taste you," Justin whispered.

Lust flared brighter in Vincent's gaze, and Vincent grasped Justin's hand, bringing it down to his straining, fabric-covered cock. Justin slid from Vincent's lap until he kneeled in front of him. Placing his hands on Vincent's thighs, Justin leaned in and mouthed at the wet spot already formed on Vincent's jeans. He didn't leave the cloth between them for long and made short work of the button and fly. The head grazed Justin's chin when he freed Vincent's stiff length. Vincent tightened his hold on the edge of the mattress when Justin locked eyes with him again and swirled his tongue over the crown, gathering the salty drop of liquid leaking from the tip.

"Fuck, Justin. So hot," Vincent moaned.

Justin wanted to see Vincent fall apart and, in an abrupt move, swallowed Vincent's cock to the root. "Holy—" Vincent's voice cracked, and he gripped Justin's head, guiding his mouth while fucking up into his throat.

Justin lashed the underside of Vincent's shaft on each retreat to the head and sucked hard on each downward motion. Wet slurping, panting moans, and harsh breathing filled the room around them, flaming their passion higher. Justin fondled Vincent's balls, rolling them in the sac, never lessening the hot pressure of his mouth.

"Justin," Vincent groaned, "if you don't stop, I'm not going to last."

Reluctantly, Justin released Vincent, but he wanted to feel Vincent inside of him. He stood and stripped. Vincent followed suit, removing his clothing. "Come here," Vincent said huskily, holding out his arms for Justin.

Justin straddled his lap again and placed his hands on Vincent's shoulders. Vincent pressed two fingers to Justin's lips. Opening his mouth, Justin accepted the digits, knowing Vincent's intent. He bathed them with saliva until they were dripping, and Vincent pulled them free. He reached behind Justin to slide first one then the other into him. Justin tilted his face toward the ceiling and closed his eyes while Vincent finger fucked him, stretching him wider until he could add a third digit. "I need you, Vincent," Justin groaned, riding Vincent's hand by rocking his hips.

"You want me here?" Vincent snarled, curling his fingers to peg Justin's prostate.

"Yes!" Justin cried.

"What do you want here, little wolf?" Vincent taunted.

"You, your cock, please," Justin begged.

Vincent replaced his fingers with his dick, the head spreading Justin and burrowing into him. Justin hissed at the feeling of being filled, widened even further, and dug his nails into Vincent's shoulders. "All right, baby?" Vincent asked.

Justin opened his eyes to look at Vincent, nodding. "God, yes."

Smirking, Vincent drove upward, impaling Justin the rest of the way onto his shaft, and Justin screamed, his body shuddering. Vincent swallowed the next sound when he took Justin's mouth with his and repeated the motion. Vincent wrapped his arms around Justin, holding him in place to plunge into him over and over. Justin couldn't stop the moans and cries falling from his lips. He slid both hands into Vincent's long hair, hanging on for dear life in the storm of pleasure he found himself swept away in.

"You feel so fucking good," Vincent growled, nipping at Justin's shoulder and throat, leaving small marks everywhere he could reach.

"Vin-ugh-Vincent," Justin howled, "I need... I need—"

"I know what you need," Vincent snarled, fucking Justin deeper and harder.

Justin's cock glided slickly between their stomachs, the tip weeping profusely. The friction and the constant stimulation of his prostate were pushing Justin closer and closer to coming. What tipped him over the edge was the loud roar Vincent let forth and the pulsing inside of him as Vincent filled him to overflowing. Justin flung his head back, shouting to the Heavens, his cock spilling between them, painting their bodies with semen.

They were both panting and trembling when their orgasms ebbed away. Justin bit back a pitiful protesting sound when Vincent pulled out of him and laid him on the bed. "Don't move," Vincent murmured.

Justin wanted to laugh. He couldn't have moved even if the apartment was on fire. His limbs felt like gelatin, and he could hardly lift his head. Vincent disappeared into the bathroom, and Justin heard the water turn on for a moment before he returned to the room. A washcloth dangled from his hand, and he tenderly cleaned Justin's backside, legs, and belly before taking care of his own mess. Vincent tossed the washcloth toward the bathroom, uncaring it hit the tile floor, and climbed into bed with Justin.

They embraced again without speaking, and the events of the day and the energy they'd just expended began to catch up to them. Within minutes, they'd both drifted off to sleep.

It wasn't until about three in the morning when Justin jackknifed in bed with a cry of, "Shit!"

Vincent jerked awake and leapt off the mattress into a fighting stance, glancing around and ready to fight. "What's wrong?"

Justin jumped out of bed and started dressing. "I have to go to Kara. I'm such an asshole. She probably thinks I'm dead."

Vincent relaxed and shook his head. "You nearly gave me a heart attack, little wolf. Give me five minutes, and I'll drive you there."

Justin paced nervously while waiting on Vincent to finish dressing. Vincent grumbled under his breath when Justin sighed with impatience; Vincent shoved his feet into his boots without lacing them and grabbed his keys. "Come on."

"Geez, you move like an old man!" Justin groused.

Vincent crowded him close to the door of his apartment and pressed their crotches together. "Does that feel like an old man to you?"

Justin grinned. "Nope."

Vincent stilled, staring at Justin with an odd look on his face. Furrowing his brow, Justin asked, "What?"

"I've never seen you smile that way before."

"What way?"

"Like you're happy."

Justin rolled his eyes and gently shoved him away enough to open the door. He jogged down the steps with Vincent following at a slower pace.

When they arrived at the house, Justin found Kara sitting slumped over the kitchen table, tear tracks staining her cheeks. Guilt stabbed him. She'd cried herself to sleep thinking he was gone. Justin ran his hand over her hair and called her name to wake her. Her eyes blinked open and, after a second of confusion, Kara leapt from her chair and snatched Justin into a hug. "Justin! Oh, my God! You didn't do it!"

"I couldn't." Justin glanced at Vincent. "I have something I have to tell you."

Pain flash over Kara's face and quickly vanished. "I kind of already figured it out."

Frowning, Justin asked, "How? Especially when I didn't even know it myself."

"I've known you ten years, Justin. You've never acted the way you do around him, never looked at someone the way you do him. The same ways I do you."

Justin winced. He'd been so blind.

Vincent stepped forward. "I want to travel with you. To help search for Jake and to end it once and for all."

She studied Vincent, an unreadable expression on her face, for several quiet moments. Then she crossed her arms and tilted her head to the side. "Well, so you know, I am not your maid. You need to clean after yourself and do your own laundry. You also have to get a job to help with the bills."

"Actually," Vincent broke in, "I don't really need to work. I have a lot of investments and also receive a stipend from the hunters' guild. None of us need to work really."

Kara and Justin looked at one another and started laughing. When they saw the bewilderment on Vincent's face, their laughter got even harder. "What is so damn funny?" Vincent demanded.

"Yo-you mean you live like that because you choose to?" they asked in unison.

"What's wrong with the way I live?" Vincent asked defensively.

Justin shook his head. "Well you definitely aren't living that way now! Come here." He wrapped one arm around Vincent and the other around Kara, hugging them close. "Welcome to the family, Vincent."

ABOUT THE AUTHOR

J.R. Loveless began her adventure in writing romance at the young age of twelve. Her foray into creating her own worlds and telling her characters' life stories was triggered by her own love of reading. She currently resides in South Florida with her dog and two cats, volunteers for an animal rescue in her spare time, and works as a manager for a financial lending institute. Someday she hopes to begin writing as a full-time career and bringing more of her ideas to life.

Her journey into gay romance began in 2005 when she began posting her original fiction on a forum for feedback and readers' pleasure. In 2010, a good friend urged her to submit to a publishing company, and the day she received the acceptance and contract was the best day of her life. Since then, she has been noted to be one of the most purchased audio books after Fifty Shades of Grey on Audiobook.com, received best gay romantic fiction for Touch Me Gently in the 2011 TLA Gaybies, and even received an award for Chasing Seth in 2012.

J.R. adores her fans and loves hearing from them.

CONNECT WITH J.R. LOVELESS

Website: www.jrloveless.com
Blog: www.jrloveless.com/blog
Facebook: https://www.facebook.com/authorjrloveless
Twitter: https://twitter.com/jrloveless
Amazon: http://amazon.com/author/jrloveless

OTHER BOOKS BY J.R. LOVELESS

Swift's Temptation

Fragments of a Unicorn's Soul

Champagne Kisses

Blue Christmas

From Dreamspinner Press:

Touch Me Gently

Chasing Seth

Forgiving Thayne

Protecting Kai

His Salvation

Love and Snowball Fights

You Belong With Me

Printed in Great Britain
by Amazon